CLAIMING HER HEART

A FERAL BREED BOOK

ELLIS LEIGH

Kinship Press

Claiming Her Heart
Copyright ©2017 by Ellis Leigh
All rights reserved
ISBN: 978-1-944336-45-5

Kinship Press
P.O. Box 221
Prospect heights, IL 60070

To those of us who like to take our time.

Okay, fine... To those who didn't straddle me for taking so damn long to write this book. Sorry.

PROLOGUE

Angelita

IF THERE WAS ONE thing I'd learned in the time since my family was slaughtered, it was that no one was safe. Not the packs, not the leaders, not mated pairs. And my mate? He was a human teenager—a blind one at that—yet he owned my heart from the moment I saw him. But I'd already lost so much. I couldn't trust the fates to keep us together, couldn't trust anyone to keep him safe. That would be my job, even though our guardians stood in our way.

I knew from the second I felt the connection between us that the next few years would be a challenge. I only hoped he was up for it, and that I had the courage to follow through in the end.

ONE

Angelita

I RACED PAST THE trees, my claws digging into the soil with every step. Running, jumping, desperate for more speed. To be closer. To reach him. To make sure he was safe. A need that never left me, never released me from its clutches. An obsession, really. Not that anyone could have blamed me for it. Not after everything I'd been through. Not since I'd found him.

My Julian.

We'd been in hell the first time we'd met. Conflict had been brewing in the shifter community, and it'd come to a head one fateful July. Enemies of the establishment, of the very thoughts and ideals our government tried to uphold, had surrounded us. Had initiated a battle to overturn the government so they could reframe our laws to better serve their own interests. My adopted family—the ones who'd taken me in after the same enemies had slaughtered my entire pack—had been in the thick of the battle, fighting for the good side. Fighting for their lives and mine.

On the night everything about shifter life and law had been under attack, I'd found my mate. My very human mate, of course, because the fates had a wicked sense of humor. Four months after a forced shift had locked me into my wolf form, when I'd still been struggling with recovering my human side, a human had come into my world and reset every expectation and desire I'd ever known. The fates must have thought it was hilarious to put a shifter girl stuck as her beast and a human man with no sight together. Must have loved making such a deep connection between two people who couldn't have been more different. Not that it mattered. He was mine.

From the moment I'd caught his scent and tracked him down in the kitchens at Merriweather Fields, to the hours of being locked in a safe room with the other youths and humans—the beings who couldn't or wouldn't fight the evil out on the lawn—I'd known. And those hours had changed me—rebuilt the fear inside of me and tore it back down. I'd struggled to stay in that moment. To not be dragged back to the memories of another battle that'd occurred on lands so very different from the Midwestern prairie-like state I'd ended up in. I'd fought past the crippling panic for one reason—Julian He'd needed me to protect him. To be his eyes for him. To watch out for him.

Our enemies had tried to start a war, and they'd failed. I would not fail Julian.

But that was then, the past. Over and done with. Today, we'd be reuniting after another separation. It'd been too long— nearly four months—since I'd been to the little house in the woods where he lived. Sixteen weeks of lonely nights and lackluster days baking under the Texas sky while Julian stayed tucked away in Michigan. Too long. Way too long. Though, visits over the past year or so had been much more frequent than at the start of our relationship.

See, the problem with being seen as a child, especially one with as brutal of a past as mine, was that everyone assumed it was their duty to protect you. I may have only been sixteen when I met my fated mate, but that didn't lessen the need to be close to him. To know where he was and what he was doing. The distance between us had been anguish, the fact that I couldn't reach the human inside of me pure destruction to my heart. I'd lived and died for the times when my mother-replacement, Sariel, would video call the sister of my mate so I could watch, so I could hear. So I could know he was okay.

Long after the night at Merriweather Fields, the one where president Blasius Zenne beat back a coup most shifters would have surrendered over, my guardians had stayed in overprotective mode. Well, one had. The other was on my side, which had caused far more problems than I'd ever intended.

"You have to let her go."

"She's a child, Sariel. A child." Bez sounded angry as he argued with his mate. Something that had been happening more often every week. Something that was my fault. "We don't know that boy, and you want me to simply send Angelita to his home and let them run amok?"

"Oh, you and your amok. Amok, amok, amok." Sariel's light footsteps came in waves, her pacing evident from where I sat huddled in a closet, eavesdropping. She only paced when she was angry. "They're mates, Bez. Just like us. They feel that connection to one another. Charlotte said Julian was beside himself when you told him he couldn't come for the Thanksgiving break."

"It's a timing issue. We're already heading up to Michigan to spend Christmas with the Feral Breed. He can wait the extra month."

There was a long silence, a drawn-out pause where nothing from the other side of the wall could give me an idea of what was happening. But silence wasn't meant to last. When Sariel spoke again, the softness of her voice, the pain behind every word, gutted me.

"She whimpers, Bez. When they have to end their computer calls. She cries for her mate."

"Sariel—"

"It's been months since they were together."

Bez's growl shocked me enough to make me back away from the wall.

"She's only sixteen," he said, the words difficult to discern beneath the rumble of his anger.

But Sariel wasn't afraid of him. I doubted there was much of anything that scared her anymore after her own experiences with the men who'd taken her. "And she's been through so much."

Bez sighed, one of those deep, frustrated ones that meant he was cracking. "Fine. Two days. We'll go up this month for two days." More silence, the creak of the floor as someone moved. Perhaps as they stepped closer to one another. "He'd better be on his best behavior. If I hear one whisper of inappropriateness—"

"She's still stuck in wolf form," Sariel said, her voice softer than before. "They'll behave."

"They'd better, or I'll kill him myself."

Biting back my snarl that night had been one of the hardest things I'd ever done. I loved Bez, I really did, but that was the night I decided things had to change. That was when I'd started plotting and practicing—scheming, even.

After that visit and the one that coincided with the human holiday of Christmas, Julian and I had spent five months apart. Five solid months of wishing we could be together but with Bez standing in our way. In preparation for the plan I had come up with—the only one I saw working to give Julian and me a future together on our own terms—I'd started sneaking out of the house. Then through the woods. Then off the compound.

The first time I'd stepped foot outside of Bez's Texas property without his permission, I'd experienced a rush of adrenaline like no other. It had pushed me on. Encouraged me. Had fed me something that would become an addiction.

The rush had also made me realize I could sneak. I could slip past the guardians around me if I needed to. And I *had* needed to.

But first, I'd needed to break through the wall between my wolf and my human side.

It had taken another eight months—long, slow months of wishing and waiting and missing my mate—for me to finally shift human. I hadn't been able to do it alone. No, I'd needed the help of an unlikely ally. A witch who was mated to one of the Feral Breed Motorcycle Club shifters. She'd jumped in to help me, and in turn, had taught me the old stereotypes shifters had about others in the shadowy world of the paranormal were just that. Stereotypes. Without Scarlett, I wouldn't have been able to move from the wolf world into the human one. I wouldn't have had a relationship with my mate. I owed her. Hugely.

Once I'd rediscovered my humanity, my sneaking around had become more focused, more direct. I'd escaped every chance I could to be able to call Julian, to use a computer to video chat with him. The town Bez lived outside of might have been small, but there was a library and two different restaurants with computers accessible. Well, technically, customers were supposed to go there during business hours and pay to rent them, but I hadn't been able to do that. So I'd found another way. I'd figured out how to tell if a building was alarmed, how to work with the wires and receivers to gain access where I wasn't supposed to be. I'd researched ways to pick locks and open locked windows, and I'd learned how to bypass simple motion detectors. I spent many hours sitting in the dark in buildings thought safe from such things, talking to the one person I was definitely supposed to be with on computers that weren't mine. I'd justified my actions with my need to see and hear Julian. He'd always been the reason, the impetus for my actions. My love for Julian had turned me into a thief. A good one.

And finally, a few years after that fight I'd listened into—months upon months of separation and struggle—I was close enough to taste my mate on the air. If only I could run faster.

Two wolves chased after me, trying to keep up. Not that they could. Not with the sort of motivation I had fueling my pace. My head filled with images of all the things that could have gone wrong since I'd been forced on to the plane. Coming north by car was easier because I had my phone. I could stay in contact with Julian. On a plane? With no Wi-Fi? Impossible. We'd been disconnected for hours, and he didn't answer the quick text I'd sent him once we landed. That wasn't like him—he always answered me. He could be hurt, taken, missing… killed.

Lost to me just like the family I'd once had.

I ducked lower, pumping my legs harder, too anxious to give up even a single second of this trek. I needed to be there, to get to him, to make sure he was okay.

The scent of shifter greeted me as I crossed the property line into Rebel's territory. Nearer now, almost there. I didn't ease my pace, though. He was just ahead, my mate; I could sense him. So close. So, so close. I raced around a stand of trees that blocked the view of the property from the street, and the house appeared, modest and glowing bright in the shadow of the forest. Small but charming, this place had been my home when I'd visited, when I had been allowed to stay close to my mate. Rebel and Charlotte's house. The one where they'd brought a son into the world just six months ago. Where little Elijah slept in his crib in what had once been my mate's room.

But what caught my attention and held it, what I couldn't look away from, was the garage. The small building out back with the staircase leading up to the second-floor apartment. The one with dark windows and no sign of life inside. Julian's home…looking empty. He had to be in the house.

Rebel opened the front door of the cottage before I reached the porch, a smile on his face.

"Good evening, Angelita."

I pushed past him as Bez and Sariel stepped onto the porch. My guardians shifted human, accepting cloaks from Rebel to hide their nakedness. I traipsed past them all and into the house, sniffing hard, pacing when I couldn't find Julian in any of the normal spots. Why wasn't he waiting for me?

"Hey, Angelita," Charlotte said as I padded into the kitchen. Baby Elijah sat on her hip, drooling and reaching for me. I loved the kid, but I had more important things to do at the moment. Had someone I desperately needed to find. I paused, looking up at Julian's sister, hoping she could tell me where to go.

"Hi, Charlotte," Sariel said as she walked in behind me. The two women greeted each other with hugs while I waited, impatient. Sariel cooed and laughed as baby Elijah reached for her, as his chubby hands met her face. She took him from his mother, both women beaming. And ignoring me.

Finally, Charlotte took pity on my whimpers. "He's in the apartment over the garage."

I took off for the door, ignoring Rebel's smirk as he held it open for me. Around the house, over the gravel driveway, and to the stairs leading up the side of the garage. How my mate traversed these every day, I had no idea. He couldn't see. And though I knew he was independent and able to do almost everything on his own, I worried. I would always worry.

When I reached the door, I jumped up, using my claws to scratch at the metal surface. Stupid round handle. If it were a lever, I could open it myself. If it weren't locked. Would he have the door locked? No, he wouldn't do anything to keep me away from him. He had to know I was here, that I was coming today. He had to—

The door swung inward, and every ounce of tension within

my body drained as my soul refocused on just one thing. One person. Julian.

I shifted human without effort, without thought, without even trying. Arms around his neck, my body pressed to his, I breathed him in. Covered him so my scent would be all over his clothes and skin. So my wolf would finally settle, knowing her mate was there.

He was safe.

He was mine.

And no one would be coming between us ever again.

I hadn't become a thief just to chat. I'd become a thief to have a future with Julian. And to hell with anyone who dared to stand in our way now.

TWO

Julian

AS AFTERNOON TURNED TO evening, I sat on the edge of the mattress, fisting the sheets to stay in place. To not go running off into the woods on a hunch, on a feeling. On the surety that I'd find Angelita. I could feel her already, sense the gap between us growing smaller with every second. She was close. Close enough that my body responded to her, my heart racing and my blood rushing to my dick.

The instinct to claim, to mate, to drive myself inside her body and join us forever wasn't just a wolf thing. I felt it, too. Always had with her. Always would.

Usually, I'd be in the house when Angelita arrived. Standing beside my sister and her husband, I'd fret and fidget until she hit the porch before I raced outside, needing to reach her right away. But this time, we needed privacy. Hell, we deserved it too. We had a lot of things to talk about. Future things, plans, all the options there were to keep us together from now on. Plus, I couldn't be so hard and needy for her in front of my sister and Angelita's guardians. There would be no hiding it this time. I'd always been able to control myself around others in the past, knowing we couldn't be together that way. Knowing I had to wait for her. But she was eighteen finally. We were adults in the eyes of the law, though not yet in the eyes of the people who had helped raise us. Still, it was time to sit down and talk as adults. To act as adults. To do…adult things.

My heart jumped the second I heard her claws on the steps outside. My Angelita was finally home. I stood, heading for the door, knowing she couldn't open it. Not like that. Not as her wolf. She must have been in a rush to have forgotten to shift. She did that sometimes still—stayed in her wolf form until the last possible second. She'd shift for me, though. Once her wolf saw me, she'd change forms.

The second her claws scraped against the steel of the door, I yanked it open. Her scent destroyed me, enveloping me completely in a nanosecond. I couldn't see her, but I didn't need to. I'd felt her coming, and I could still feel her. Feel the pull to her that was something I'd never quite gotten used to. Feel the way she made my heart burn when she was close to me. The pull to grab her, hold her, leave not an inch of space between us. I could smell her, hear her breath, feel the energy rolling off her… Carnal and wild. She was my angel, my soul mate, my love. Everything I needed in life was wrapped up in her little body. I didn't need my sight to recognize her—I knew every bit of her without ever having to see an inch.

Her fur brushed along my legs, and I smiled, the sensation tickling. The next second, skin replaced fur, and my amazing Angelita wrapped her human form around my body. Her naked human form. This girl tested every ounce of my willpower and always had.

"Leelee." My nickname for her came out on a sigh of its own accord. I couldn't have held it back any more than I could stop my body from responding to hers. I grabbed her close, loving the feel of warm, soft skin under my hands. Breathing in the scent of rain and forest and girl. So much girl.

No… *Woman.*

"Julian." Her shaky, whispered voice saying my name broke me. I grabbed her legs, hoisting them up around my waist and slammed the door behind her. This woman, this amazing, beautiful, soulful woman knew exactly how to push me past my limits in all the best ways, and I would never be separated from her again. I'd battle the whole shapeshifter population if I had to. She was mine.

Diving in, I kissed her roughly, all teeth and smashed lips as I dug my fingers into her thighs to hold her to me. I walked backward until my legs hit the mattress again, then dropped down, pulling Angelita into my lap. Letting her wrap herself around me and straddle my hips. Fuck, I'd never been so hard. Never been so needy for her. We'd gotten good at kissing over the years—once she'd been able to shift human again, we'd done everything we could to catch up on the time we'd lost. We'd taken advantage of every second together because we knew Bez could tear us apart again if he wanted to. We'd spent hours on each visit kissing, hugging, rubbing…exploring. But we'd never gone too far. Never crossed the line into anything more than hands on one another. She'd been underage, and I'd been threatened too many times to slip.

But she was eighteen now, and somehow, my body knew it.

The kiss grew hotter, deeper. Her body pressed into mine as I dragged my hands over her back and cupped her ass. My fingers sank into her flesh, rocking her against me. Letting her feel how hard I was for her, how much I wanted her. How she drove me insane with desire. I thrust upward, letting my length drag against where she was so hot and warm for me. Teasing her in a way I knew she liked until she was a gasping, whimpering pile of need.

Our kiss—our movements—were far more passionate and bold than they'd ever been before. I felt it—she had to as well.

Four months apart had left us both too close to the edge, but this was it. Our last reunion after such a separation. We'd never be apart again as long as I had a say in it. I just had to convince her of one last thing. Just had to get her to accept the future we'd been hurtling toward since the day we met.

But first, I needed to make her come. It'd been way too long for both of us.

Angelita pushed me back, leaning down to nuzzle my neck. To place small bites along the length of it as I moaned beneath her. She laid her scent down on me, claiming me as hers to the rest of the animals. Such a wolf thing to do, but I loved it. Craved it, really.

Her animal side probably shouldn't have turned me on as much as it did, but I couldn't help it. She drove me wild all the time. Her human, her wolf, every part of her called to parts of me. Enticed me closer. She sang a siren song only for me, and I was more than willing to plunge to my death on her rocky shore.

Once done with my neck, Angelita backed up so she could place a hard bite right over my heart. Even through my shirt, I felt the sting of her teeth. Felt the way she held back. She wanted to bite harder, deeper—to break the skin and make our claiming permanent. I sensed it, right along with her fear of such a thing. Her hesitation.

Not mine—never mine. Only hers. I was ready to join her in every way, but she wasn't. A sticking point for us.

When she finished with her love bites, Angelita straddled my hips again, lining up her soft and wet with my hard and straining. Another kiss, softer, a lick of my lips, and then she rocked, dragging her flesh against the fabric of my shorts. If we were naked, I'd be inside her already. I'd be...

"Fuck, Leelee." I gripped her thighs and threw my head back, lost to the sensations. I wanted her, wanted to push inside her body, wanted to discover what that felt like, how tight and wet and hot she'd be. How soft. I'd experienced her with my fingers and lips, but not my dick. Not yet. But I wanted her, had since the first time she'd shifted human and went from being my wolf-pal Angelita to my mate Leelee. Had for way longer than was probably acceptable, but I didn't care. She'd always been mine.

As the scent of her arousal made me groan louder and longer with every push, Angelita rocked harder, a growl rumbling through her chest as her fingers dug into my shoulders. That growl meant she was close to coming. Meant her body was taking over her thoughts. I loved that sound. Loved feeling her come on some part of my body, knowing I did that. That I'd always be the one to give that pleasure to her.

"Jul," she hissed, her thighs tightening around my hips, her hands pushing against my chest as she writhed over me. I thrust up harder, craving her so much, desperate to be inside her. Desperate to join us forever in every way. To claim her as mine and let her claim me right back. To come inside her so every other wolf knew she belonged to a male already.

I wasn't stupid—I knew there were shifters after her. Wanting to fuck her. I didn't have to see her body to feel the litheness of it, the gentle curves. I knew she was beautiful too. But I also knew how she sounded when she came, how much she liked her nipples bitten instead of sucked, how sweet she tasted when I crawled between her thighs. I knew...and I wasn't fucking sharing.

"Julian, missed you so much. Missed...this. I'm...I'm..." Angelita clenched down hard, her hands gripping my shoulders as her entire body went stiff over me. Fuck, so hot. So amazing. So...

"Mine." Yanking her down so I could swallow her cries, I came with a groan, my come wet and warm on my stomach. My hands like steel on her hips as I pulled her tighter and licked into her mouth. As we calmed down enough to slow our movements until we were practically still once more.

When I had caught my breath, I kissed her little nose. "Missed you too, Leelee."

My angel giggled as she rolled off me to snuggle into my side. Still so warm and naked. I loved the feel of her skin under my hands, loved the way she reacted to my touch. I kissed the top of her head, holding her close, tingles still shooting up my spine. This sort of cuddling was our thing, our favorite way to pass the time. Snuggled together as we'd been doing since before she'd found her human side, though never before with her naked. That fact added a hotness to the act I'd once thought of as innocent. How could I not when I'd started it with an animal instead of a human?

That first year—the one between when we'd met and when she'd finally shifted human—had been one of the strangest of my life. Not only had I learned there were such things as witches and shapeshifters in the world, but I'd also met Angelita and been told the fates had brought us together to be mated. I hadn't thought it possible—what was I going to do with a wolf? But the connection to her, the need to be around her, the deep understanding that she was mine and I was hers—it was all too strong to ignore. So I'd fallen in love with a wolf. And that day when she'd finally found her human side—after so long of having her in my life as practically a pet—I'd understood what lust was.

"I don't like flying. I don't want to do it again without you." Head on my shoulder, she sucked on my neck. Nipping, licking, teasing me again. This girl would be my heaven and my hell, my impossible lust and my satiation. Forever.

I groaned, grabbing her hip and pulling her closer. Already hard for her again. Needing so much more but knowing she'd throw up walls if I brought it up. If I even mentioned completing the mating claim. Not just exchanging bites to link our souls, but letting her share her wolf with me. Giving myself over to her world and leaving my human one behind. She'd refused to even talk about it as an option since the moment we'd met without getting upset. I wasn't ready for that just yet.

So instead, I pulled her closer and took advantage of our alone time with my wandering hands. "Never without me. Got it."

If I had my way, she'd never go anywhere without me again.

The rest of the shifters had always said they'd known their mates the second they saw them. Hell, even my human sister had felt a pull to her mate immediately—one she'd tried hard to deny. Tried and failed, thank God, because otherwise, I never would have met Angelita.

But still, every story had been "at first sight." Being blind, I'd thought Angelita and I would never get that full connection. I'd been wrong. The second my hands had touched her human skin, I'd known she was mine. I'd grown hard in an instant, had wanted to sink my teeth and my dick inside her right that second. Not that I'd acted on it. I'd restrained myself, even when she'd whimpered as if feeling the same drive to bond that I had.

That need had become brighter, hotter as the months passed. We'd gone from stolen moments over the phone simply chatting or sitting in silence to whispered late-night admissions of what we wanted to do to one another and texts I had to use my headphones to listen to because of what they said. Leelee also liked to video chat with me, which we did quite often. Her voice would brighten when she could see me, a fact I loved. That was my doing. Making my mate, my woman, happy with a simple video call.

But we relegated calls and texts to the back burner whenever we ended up together. Every visit, we became more daring. More connected. More…lustful. We wouldn't be virgins for much longer. She was pushing me more and more, and I wanted to take our relationship to that point. I wanted her. Fuck, did I want her. I wanted her forever, and that meant she needed to give me something more than her body. We needed to complete our mating, and she needed to give me a piece of her inner animal. Something the two of us couldn't compromise on.

"Want you," she mumbled, her lips tickling my skin. Her hips rolling against mine in a seductive dance that almost broke me.

Almost, but not quite. Still, I gripped her hips hard and let out a groan. "We can't yet."

"Why not?" Her voice had gone whiny, her need taking over. Pushing me. But I was ready for that. I needed to hold back, no matter how difficult she made it.

So I took a deep breath and held her still. "You know why."

Angelita stopped, pulling away as I knew she would. This wasn't the first time we'd had this conversation. The one where I asked her to bite me, to mark me, to complete our mating claim so later she could turn me into a shifter like her. She always shut me down quickly, but I would initiate the conversation again once I felt enough time had passed. I'd hoped this time would be the last—that she'd finally accept the need for this to have the future we deserved—but the tension in her body made me doubt my chances of success. Angelita stood totally against turning me. I knew that, and I had yet to figure out a way to change her mind.

Fear made her skin go cold, made her voice too shaky. "I won't."

I sighed, rubbing my hands up and down her arms. "Lee—"

"No," she snapped. "I won't. We can exchange mating bites, but I won't turn you into a shapeshifter, Julian."

"Why not? You know changing me would give us even more time together. Completing the mating bite will slow my aging, but I'll still surpass you every year. We won't have forever mated, but we might if I'm like you. Why would you deny us that?"

She paused, and when she finally spoke, it wasn't my Angelita anymore. Gone was the brave, wild girl who demanded my attention. In her place was someone quiet, meek...terrified. Someone who pulled away and left me alone in the bed.

"What if I do it wrong? I've never been a wolf giver. What if I make a mistake, and you don't come through it? What if your mind can't handle the turning? I don't want to lose any part of you."

"You won't." I reached for her, but she walked away. The alternating volume of her footsteps indicated she was pacing the length of the room. Back and forth, back and forth. Stressed.

"How do you know?" she whispered. "How can you be so sure your turning won't end in disaster?"

"Because I have faith in you. In us and our future." I stood, reaching for her again, finally circling her wrist with my fingers. I tugged her closer, wrapped my arms around her hips. Kissed the center of her chest before pulling her against me. "I trust you and our families to make sure we do this right."

She ran her fingers through my hair and sighed.

"I trust no one, especially not myself."

THREE

Angelita

I CLUNG TO JULIAN'S hand as we walked toward the cottage where Rebel and Charlotte lived, the clothes I'd borrowed from him hanging loosely on my body. But it wasn't the baggy shorts or too-big tee that made my skin feel too tight. For as many years as I'd been able to shift human again, being in this form still made me uncomfortable. I always felt weaker, more exposed. I'd been ambushed once while human and lost…well, everything. I'd been stuck human while trapped on a houseboat in a swamp with men who made my skin crawl, who my wolf would have gladly fought against if she'd been able to take over. Instead, I'd been forced to wait for someone to rescue me, and thank the fates someone had. Two someones. If it hadn't been for Bez and Sariel, my saviors and guardians, I'd probably be dead.

Gripping Julian's hand tighter, I took a deep breath to calm myself. Not again. I wouldn't lose my mate. He was human, blind, and at a total disadvantage from an attack. I had to take care of him.

My wolf growled inside my head, watchful and wary. She hated when I wouldn't let her out. It was so hard to find the balance between her and my human side at times. She'd hurt and lost just as much as I had when those bastards had come to steal me away. She didn't like being forced to sit back and watch as I traversed the world on two legs. If it were up to her, my human side would never come out again. She'd tuck that weaker self into her den and protect it with teeth and claws for as long as we lived, letting out the Omega power she bore when needed. But then we'd lose Julian, and that wasn't an option. So I pushed her back, caging her inside my human mind as much as I could.

My wolf huffed, an angry sort of snort only I could hear. I knew what she wanted, but it wasn't her time. It was human Angelita time…no matter how anxious that made us both.

Sariel opened the door as we reached the back porch. Her smile was bright and wide as she looked us over, making sure we were whole and healthy. She always did that to me—looked me up and down, sniffing, checking. I knew it was because she'd been in the same nightmare boat as I had. Literally. Though her family and former pack lived, she was still taken from them. Stolen away like a piece of property and threatened with horrors too great to think about. Sariel's mate had saved me, saved her as well, and I'd been with them ever since. Bez kept us safe, tucked away in what was essentially a fortress in Texas. But even a fortress could be breached with the right motivation and information. I knew because I'd broken in and out of it numerous times. Which was how I knew my plan would work. If I could only find the right opportunity. The right time to try. To show all of them I could handle myself without constant protection.

"Rebel is just finishing up with some company," Sariel said as she leaned against the doorframe. "Are you two hungry?"

I loved both of my adopted parents, but especially Sariel. There was a sweet sort of strength to her. While Bez was tactical and brutal, Sariel was nurturing and kind. A second mother for sure. Not that I'd ever told her that. I'd loved my family as well, had told them nearly every day, and they'd been ripped away from me. I couldn't risk it again.

I shook my head, giving Julian's hand a squeeze. "I'm not. Are you?"

"I can always eat." He'd never said such truer words. I had no idea how many times he'd had to pause one of our conversations over the years so he could grab a snack.

We followed Sariel into the house, walking into the bright kitchen from the back mudroom. My wolf growled low in my mind, alerting me to the presence of others. Of people we didn't know. Rebel had never handled business at his home before, a fact that snagged my curiosity.

"Why don't you grab a snack?" I said, focusing on Julian so I didn't alert Sariel to my plan. "I'm going to use the bathroom."

He froze, facing me, seeming to watch me even though I knew he couldn't see. I may have been able to pull the wool over Sariel's eyes, but Julian was too aware of me and his other senses to trick.

I rose up as if to kiss his cheek and whispered, "I just want to see who else is here."

He squeezed my hand, accepting, warning.

"I know," I said, then backed away. "I'll be right back."

Sariel began chatting with Julian, unknowingly making my efforts to sneak into the living room—or close enough to see and hear what was going on—that much easier. I slipped around the corner and down the hall, heading for the guest room at the back of the house. Most people would have tried to sneak into the hallway, maybe hide around the corner there to eavesdrop. I wasn't most people. See, the little house on the island had forced air heat, meaning there were vents in every room. There happened to be one that was used to return cold air to the furnace at the far side of the living room. It connected to the air return in the guest room. If I lay on the floor, it would be as if I were in the same room as Rebel and whoever had come to talk to him.

So I lay on the floor, and I inched close enough to press my ear to the metal grate.

"I told you, it's just not what we do." Rebel—his distinct voice and slight accent gave him away.

"I'll pay well. This artifact is important to my clan. We're desperate to get it back."

Recovery of an item? That piqued my interest for sure, made me want to know more. Want to jump through the wall and volunteer to handle the mission, but I couldn't. Not with Rebel and Bez involved. They'd never let me do what I wanted to. Never understand or accept my skills, the ones I just knew would lead to independence if given the shot. A lost artifact sure seemed like a shot to me.

I peeked through the grate, squinting as I tried to get a visual on the other speaker for future reference. He stood close to the door, his back to me. Shoot. All I could tell was he was huge—tall and broad in a way most humans were not. Neither were wolves, usually.

"As I said," Rebel started, his voice dropping and his growl evident. "The Feral Breed Motorcycle Club doesn't deal in recovering stolen items. There's nothing we can do for you, and I'd appreciate it if you got the fuck out of my house."

The man sighed. "I apologize for disturbing you. Thank you for your time."

He turned, his gray overcoat lifting slightly as he did. That move gave me just enough of an angle to get a good look— tall, with dark red hair, and a thick, full beard. The man stood at least a full head taller than Rebel and was nearly twice as wide. More muscular than the wolf shifter. He'd said clan, so he had to be a bear shifter. I'd met a few in Texas once during an investigation Bez headed up. They'd always seemed nice enough—wary of wolves and a little on the quiet side, but nothing overtly aggressive or dangerous. Except for their size. Those shifters were mammoth even in human form.

So a bear shifter was looking to retrieve an artifact that was important to his clan and had come to ask the Feral Breed for help. Important meant valuable, and that meant money. Maybe the bear was willing to pay a fee. If he were…other people would be. Paranormal people. The sort that couldn't go to a regular detective or inspector. Ideas and concepts shot through my mind, wispy but with potential. If I could solidify something, one problem in my life would be solved. I'd just need to look for a chance, for my opportunity to talk to the bear without anyone else around.

I needed to make a plan.

Rebel closed the door behind the bear shifter just as the guest room door swung open. I jumped to my feet, but Julian just raised a finger to his lips and beckoned me. Something I could never resist.

"So?" he whispered as the warmth of his body against mine and the feel of his breath on my skin made me break out in goose bumps. I ran my hands up his arms, pulling him closer so I could reply. Rubbing my nose up his neck and scenting him simply because I could. He smelled so good, so strong and masculine. I wanted to lick him up one side—

He patted my ass as my tongue flicked against his skin, chuckling softly to get my attention back where it should be.

"Right. Yeah. So, bear shifter looking for the Feral Breed to retrieve something that's important to his clan."

"Huh. That's not what the club does."

I closed my eyes, relishing the warmth of my mate. "That's what Rebel told him."

Julian hummed and dropped his head to place a soft kiss

on my shoulder. While cuddling the way we were was definitely my favorite way to talk, it was also a necessity. In a house filled with wolf shifters whose animal senses tended to be far stronger than average human ones, privacy was next to impossible.

Something made all too clear when Sariel's voice carried down the hall. "Break it up, you two."

"Busted," I whispered, letting the air hiss over my lips. Julian grinned and grabbed my ass again.

"Worth it." He dragged me out into the hall, holding my hand as he did so there was more room between us. Not that I wanted room. In fact, I wanted the opposite of room. I wanted to join with him as mates were supposed to. We'd put off our claimings for so long, following human rules and laws to appease those around us. I was so done with all that, but Julian wanted more than I was ready to give him. An endless source of frustration, for sure.

"Angelita, can you do me a favor?" Sariel wrestled a bin of cans and bottles from its usual place under the sink. "Can you take out the recyclables? Charlotte will be done feeding the baby at any minute, and she never lets me help her clean up."

I reached for the bin, but Julian beat me to it.

"I've got it, Miss Sariel. Thanks for helping my sister."

Sariel caught my eye, grinning. "You're welcome, Julian. I'm happy to help."

"I'll grab the door for you." I jumped in front of Julian. The scent of woods and water greeted me again as I stepped outside, but they didn't soothe me. No, as Julian walked lightly down the steps and toward where the garbage was stored, those scents tormented me. I rushed to keep up with my mate, opening the lid on the recyclable container and guiding him so he could empty the bin.

"Done," I said, letting the lid fall. "Let's get back inside."

"Quit stressing," Julian whispered, allowing me to nearly pull him back to the house. "I can feel your thoughts from here."

"I'm just a little—"

"Worried. Yeah, I know. You're always worried when we're outside." He led me forward, dragging me away from the kitchen and toward a storage room at the back of the house once we were inside the door. Tucked away in the shadows, I spun, growling, fighting back the instinct to shift. To take. To claim him as mine right then and there. It was so hard to resist him, so difficult to go against the pull between us. To deny what we both needed.

Julian shut the door to the storage room and grabbed me, lifting me off the ground, pulling me into his arms. I settled immediately, the feel of his skin on mine a balm like no other. Wrapped around my mate was exactly where I wanted to be. Forever.

"Relax. You're so worked up right now." Julian's lips met mine in a slow, soft kiss. One that stole my breath. "We're here, we're safe, I won't let anything happen to you."

I pressed my forehead to his chest, holding tight to him, soothing myself with the sound of his heart. "I know."

"No, you don't. But you will. Eventually." He kissed the top of my head and set me down. "Now, let's go see that brute of a father of yours."

"He's not my father."

"Could have fooled me." We walked out together, hand in hand. Normal except for the scratchy need tormenting me from under my skin. Game-face time.

"Julian, Angelita, come join us." Rebel smiled at us from where he sat on the edge of a chair. His mate, Charlotte, sat in the chair, looking almost dwarfed by the way the shifter had basically draped himself across her shoulders. I hid my smirk, my wolf knowing it was a power-play move on Rebel's part. There was another Alpha male in the house, one big and bad enough to threaten Rebel in his own den. He rarely left Charlotte's side when Bez was anywhere near, even though Bez was happily mated to Sariel. Silly male wolves and their need to be the top dog at all times.

I led Julian to the open couch, directly across from Bez. Sariel tried to sit beside him, but he yanked her onto his lap with a growl. Wolf posturing from him as well.

"I'm glad you're both here," Charlotte said, sitting forward. "There're a few things we'd like to talk about."

Julian stiffened beside me. "Char."

I glanced from brother to sister, almost tasting the tension between them. My wolf crept forward in my mind, watching Charlotte, not happy that she was upsetting our mate. Our protective streak was wide and never-ending, even in regards to family.

Charlotte must have felt the wolfish energy of my glare. She sat back again, eyeing me hard. "There are things that need to be discussed."

"What things?" I asked on a growl.

"Well, like plans. What are you two going to do now that you're…adults?"

I glanced at Julian and squeezed his hand, not wanting to step over him and declare anything, seeing as it was his family doing the asking this time.

"We're going to stay together," he said simply. I nodded, knowing that was what I wanted as well.

Charlotte seemed to expect that answer. "And what about college?"

Julian huffed. "There's time for that."

"Julian, Mom and Dad—"

"Don't," he interrupted, his voice hard. "Don't invoke our

parents just because you think your life would have been better if they'd been alive."

"Julian," Rebel warned.

"No, I get it. Mom and Dad died, and I lost my sight. It was horrible, a tragedy, and saintly Charlotte gave up everything to keep me with her and raise me to do all the things she never got to." Julian sat forward, his hand shaking in mine. "I'm not you, though, Char. The one thing I want is the one thing you fought hardest against. I want to be with Angelita, to experience the love of soul mates, to live our lives together, and be happy. Forever."

Charlotte frowned, staring at her brother with sad eyes. "You can still do that and go to college."

"Really? And how do we pull that off? Angelita's never been in a human school. She'll never be able to keep the secret of what she is in that sort of setting. She hates crowds, doesn't get along well with strangers, and would never be comfortable in a campus environment."

My stomach dropped, guilt a heavy burden on my heart. "I can blend."

Julian spun toward me, probably hearing the hurt in my voice. "But that's the thing. I don't want you to blend. I don't want you to try to tame yourself for other people one damn bit. I love your wolfishnish. I want you to be comfortable with where we live."

"I can be comfortable in the human world." Which was a lie. I couldn't, and luckily, Julian knew it.

"You'd be worried all the time, and I'd end up worried about you worrying so much. We'd be much happier together—away from the crowds of humans who would never understand how special and amazing you are. We'd fit better into the shifter world than the human one."

I melted into his side, practically purring. "You're sort of the sweetest."

He kissed my head. "Just sort of?"

"Julian." Charlotte wasn't just frowning anymore. She looked angry. Julian had to have heard the harsher tone in her voice, because he stiffened. And, no matter how unlikely it was, I swear I heard my mate growl.

"What?" His voice sounded just as harsh as hers, though his carried a tone of dismissal. This was going to go badly for both of them, I could already feel it coming.

Charlotte's eyes flashed my way. "I need you to be serious."

"I am serious. I want to live my life with Angelita. I want the two of us to be happy. Why isn't that enough?"

"Angelita?" Bez asked, his husky voice breaking the tension between the siblings. "What do you want?"

I glanced from Julian to his sister, then back to the man who'd taken on the responsibility of raising me. He gave nothing away with his expression, but I knew him. Knew how much he believed in the sanctity of a mating bond. Knew how hard it'd been on him these years as I left his home for Rebel's to stay close to my mate, to give up protecting me for those weeks every year. He hadn't wanted me to grow up too fast or to be without his insane level of protection, but he would never try to stand in our way now. Not after everything—not since I'd become an adult in the eyes of even the humans. And I knew, no matter what I chose, he'd be right behind me. Backing me up the way only he could. With brute strength and a will as strong as steel.

Even if he disagreed with my decision.

That fact gave me the courage to lay my heart and soul on the line in front of everyone. "He's my mate, and I love him. I want to live here, with him."

Bez stared at me, eyes hard, before he finally nodded. "It's what they want."

Charlotte's face went red. "But what will they do for money?

And what about college? Julian's only a year in—he needs to finish that degree."

"We'll get to all that," Julian said. "I can go local or do most of my classes online. I'm not saying I'm dropping out, but I'm not going away to live the college campus life. It's not for me, and it's certainly not for Angelita." Julian pulled me into his side, resting his hand on my hip. "I'm not giving everything up, and that includes the life I want with my mate. We have time to deal with the rest."

I met Sariel's eyes. They mirrored the emotions I felt roiling under the surface. Worry, fear, anxiety. Sariel had been trapped on that damned houseboat right along with me, for far longer than I'd been. She could have died there. We both had a deep and personal understanding of how wrong Julian could be.

Sometimes time was the one thing you didn't have.

"And what about you, Julian?" Rebel asked. "Do you want to become a wolf shifter?"

Julian answered yes at the same moment I blurted out a no. Typical.

"We still have a few decisions to make," Julian said, his hand squeezing mine. His voice tight.

Rebel raised an eyebrow. "Might want to lock that decision down before you exchange mating bites, then."

Charlotte spun, her mouth agape. "Abraham."

"What?" Rebel shrugged. "They're mates, and there's no denying their souls are ready for the next step. It would be irresponsible of us not to remind them of the commitment such a thing entails."

"We know." Damn, did we know. "We won't be jumping into anything without more discussions."

Rebel and Bez both looked as if they doubted my words, Charlotte seemed disappointed, but Sariel? She simply smiled, her red-rimmed eyes giving her away. I'd be leaving her home, which meant her job as my mother was done. And given the fact that she couldn't bear children of her own, that had to be a difficult truth to accept. But I wouldn't bring Julian to Texas—he and Bez would never get along well enough for that. I needed to stay put, to learn to live in the Midwest if I wanted to stay close to my mate. Which I did. Enough to be willing to leave behind the woman who'd saved my life.

FOUR

Julian

"I THOUGHT FOR SURE your sister would have put up more of a fight about us shacking up together." Angelita gave my hand a squeeze before walking toward the bathroom of my apartment. I crossed the room, thankful to be alone with her. We'd retreated from the main house after dinner, neither of us wanting to deal with the tension between our two sets of non-parental units. We needed quiet and peace, and to talk some more. Just the two of us.

I reached the end of the bed and sat down, remembering the tone of Charlotte's voice when she'd finally agreed with Bez. "I'm sure she's not quite done yet, but the worst is probably over."

The sound of water running was my only answer, and I counted until it stopped. Eight seconds to silence, three more as she reached for the towel, and then the rustle of fabric as she dried her face. Angelita never understood how in tune with her I was. How much I knew about what she was doing and feeling just by the sounds she made, by the smell of her, by the tone of her voice. I couldn't see her emotions expressed, but I felt them. Strongly and deeply.

The click of the light going off had me cocking my head.

Angelita padded across the floor toward me, bringing her warm, earthy smell with her. Want burned deep and strong inside of me, need. My mate and I were about to sleep together in the same bed for the first time, and I was wound tight in anticipation of feeling her against me all night long.

When it seemed to take forever for her to get to me, I reached out, needing to touch her, too impatient to wait until she crawled into bed with me. It took a second, but I finally grasped her hand with mine, immediately pulling her on top of me, rolling her to the side so she lay between my body and the wall. Protecting her from the rest of the world. Wanting to hide her away.

"What's gotten into you?" she asked with a laugh. That joy, that ease—I craved it all the time. I wanted her happy and relaxed, wanted her animal side to be comfortable no matter where we were.

I shrugged, nuzzling into her neck in a mimic of the way she always did to me. "Your scent."

"My scent?" Fuck, her words came out a little softer, a little rougher. Her smell changed, deepening with arousal as she curled into my body. I knew that scent. I loved that scent. My body responded, sending my blood to my already hardening cock, throwing my heart into overdrive.

We were alone…for the entire night.

"Yeah, it's calling to me. I need more of it." I ran my hands over her back, pulling her closer the lower I went. Pressing my fingers deep into her flesh as I moved below her waist. Skin welcomed me, warm, soft, not enough and too much at the same time. Cotton and lace slid over the backs of my hands as I reached lower, as I moved under her clothes. As I craved. "Damn, Leelee. You're driving me crazy here."

She moaned this time instead of giggling, creeping closer as I kneaded the flesh of her ass. "I try."

"You succeed." I gripped her tight, melding my mouth with hers. Fuck, my chest hurt. There was a pressure, a need deep within me to join with this woman. Something I hadn't felt before. I wanted to do more than love on her, wanted to go beyond my lips against hers and my hands all over her. I wanted to take her. To join us together forever as mates. To fuck and bite and claim—to give in to what I'd resisted for so long—to give myself to the woman the fates deemed my perfect match.

That same need had always been present, but it'd simmered at first. Barely more than a warm breath when I would hear Angelita's voice or smell her scent. It'd grown over the years since we met, building higher, burning brighter. And hotter. So fucking hot.

My Angelita wasn't a timid girl. She rolled me onto my back, moving in concert with me, straddling my hips with her hands against my chest. "We're alone."

The pressure, the heat. This girl was such a tease. And I loved it. I rocked her over me, shifting until we were lined up exactly as I wanted us to be. Well, not quite exactly. There were still too many layers between us. "I know."

"So," she said, sitting up and moving her hips in a way that made me groan. Made me need. "What do you want to do?"

"I don't know. Watch a movie?" I tried to keep my voice calm, almost detached to match hers, but it was so hard. As was I. Angelita rocked on top of me, dragging her pussy over my cock. The heat from her, the pressure—it was too much and not enough all at the same time. I kept my hands on her hips, guiding her, lifting my hips to match her rhythm as we moved. This wasn't new. I'd felt her come before like this, heard her little gasps and fell apart at her satisfied moans. This, we were good at.

"Huh," she said, almost gasping the word. "I… Oh, God… I wonder what's…on."

No, she didn't. Her breath sped up, the warmth between her legs growing. She rocked harder, snapping her hips faster. Releasing a gasp every few strokes as I pushed against her. She wasn't wondering anything except when I was going to make her come. And I hated to keep her waiting.

Without a word, I rolled us both, caging her in with my arms as my hips settled between her legs.

She squealed, holding on to me, sounding pouty as she said, "No fair."

"Sure, it is." I lined my cock up with where she was so wet for me and rolled my hips. She shivered, clinging to my shoulders. Breathing out a deep sigh as I picked up where we'd left off. I dropped my weight onto her a little more, knowing she liked that. Knowing how much she felt protected and cared for when I surrounded her. Angelita hitched her leg over my hip and opened herself wider for me. *One of these days*—I grunted, trying to hold back as my thoughts swirled to things we had yet to experience. We'd been naked around each other already. I'd felt every inch of her—kissed each one, too. We'd managed to find time to do the things most people our age did. Except for one.

Pumping my hips, grunting with every stroke, I let my mind conjure up how it would feel to push inside my mate. Tried to imagine what all that soft, warm, wet flesh enveloping mine would be like. The base of my spine started to tingle, and my arms shook. Fuck, I wanted her. Wanted to know every part, to discover ourselves together in all ways. She'd been my first kiss, my first love. She was mine, but sex meant something more to a shapeshifter like my Angelita. It meant mating, claiming, and—if she lost control—biting. I couldn't wait for that day. Angelita was too afraid of the bite to be as excited as I was. It was a point of contention with no compromise, and one we'd been discussing for months.

"Please, Julian."

Angelita's breathy plea brought me back to the moment. I refocused on her, centered myself, and picked up my pace. My girl was needy, shaking beneath me as she climbed toward her release. I wanted to give that to her. Needed to. Those moments when she cried out her satiation were some of my favorites and, knowing I did that for her, some of my proudest. I growled low and dark, dropping my head to her shoulder. Fuck, I was going to come in my pants, without anything more than a bump and grind. I tried to stop, I really did, but she felt so good. So warm. And I knew she was so wet for me.

"I can't…" The words wouldn't come. I wanted to tell her I couldn't wait, couldn't last. Couldn't resist her. Luckily, she knew. She always knew.

"So close." She growled darkly, her hips pressing against mine. Her entire body wrapping around me as her nails dug into my back. I knew her tells, could feel her growing tight and fluttering where I pressed against her. Not long now. I had to hold on. Had to get her there. Fuck, I had to make her come first. Always.

Digging deep for any wisp of control I had left, knowing she liked it when I talked a little dirty to her, I whispered, "C'mon, Leelee. I want to know how wet you're going to get tonight. Let me feel you come against my cock."

She gasped, her muscles clenching, her entire body going stiff as pleasure broke over her. I froze for just a moment, sinking into the sensations of her orgasm. The sound of her stuttered breath, the near pain of her claws slipping out and pressing into the flesh of my back, the pulse of her pussy against me, the scent of her slickness teasing me with what I wanted to feel and taste. Glorious. Perfect. Fucking mine.

I thrust against her one last time and followed her over that edge. Grunting through my own release as I pressed her into the mattress. There was no stopping, no holding back. I came hard and long, collapsing just to the side of my girl as I finally came back from the depths of pleasure.

Angelita curled around me when we were quiet once more, her body warm and pliant beneath my hands. "We really should do that without clothes in the way."

I chuckled and sighed. "You know we can't."

"We can," she said, running her nose along my cheek. "I want to."

"But if you lose control and bite me—"

"We'll be mates."

"Right, but that's not enough." I ran my hands over her curves, wishing she'd see things my way just this once. "We're mates now, and I know claiming each other is the next step. But then what? I stay human and get left behind?"

"I wouldn't—"

"Mean to. You wouldn't mean to, but you would. Every time you went for a run in the woods, every time you shifted wolf in your sleep like you do. Every single moment of your life you'd be different from me because of your wolf side, and I don't want that. I want to know my forever is the same as yours."

"Julian—"

"I want you to turn me into a wolf shifter." The words escaped without thought, without care. My biggest want, my most desperate need, laid bare before Angelita. And I knew exactly how she'd answer.

As expected, Angelita stiffened, trying to pull away. "I can't."

"You can," I said as I gripped her, refusing to let her back away from the conversation we needed to have. "I know you can."

Her hands pulled me closer, tugging hard at my shoulders. Fear making her grabby. "I can't lose you, too. I won't do it."

Pain. Dread. Those were the things holding her back. I understood her reservations—she'd watched her entire family, her entire pack, be slaughtered. She'd lost everything. I understood, all right, but that didn't make her refusal any easier to accept. "You won't lose me, Leelee. I'll come through and be just like you."

"You could die or go mad. I won't do it."

I pulled back, my forehead against hers. Wishing I could see her face as I whispered, "It's what I want, Lee. It's the future I've chosen for myself." Time to show my hand. "If you won't do this for me, I'll get Gates or one of the other guys to do it."

I smelled her tears before I heard her gasp, knew she was crying by the way her body went soft even before that.

"You won't lose me," I whispered, holding her tighter. "Trust the fates to keep us together forever."

Angelita shook her head. "The fates did nothing to save my family. I can't trust them."

"Trust *me*, then."

She lay silent for a long time. I could almost sense her eyes on me, could imagine her watching me as she contemplated our future. I tried to stay calm, to remain steadfast, but this issue always upset the two of us. There was no middle ground for us. She wanted me human, and I didn't.

"I don't know if you can beat death," she whispered, her tears coming harder.

I kissed her lips and wiped away the wetness on her cheeks. As frustrating as it was to be caught within her fear cycle, I could never blame her. I would always take care of her. "And that right there is why we can't go further, Lee. You don't trust me enough, which means there are cracks in our connection."

"No, it's not that."

"Yeah, it is." I rolled off the bed, heading for my dresser to grab a clean pair of sweats. "I want you, Angelita. Every day. Forever. I don't want to miss a single experience with you. I want to laugh with you, want to be intimate with you, and yes,

I want to run in wolf form with you. I want to be able to take adventures with you. But you just want to keep me in a box, all locked up and as safe as you can make me."

The bed squeaked behind me, and the sheets rustled in a way that told me she was sitting up. "Why is it wrong to want you safe?"

"Because life isn't safe, and I want to live it. You lost your family, and so did I. Yes, I got to keep my sister, but I lost my parents. I lost a lot of my independence too. But I refuse to give up or give in." I headed for the bathroom, needing a break. Needing a moment. But not before I said my piece. "There is nothing we can't do so long as we're together, Leelee. I just wish you had enough faith in me to believe that."

I shut the bathroom door behind me and stood there, listening. Trying not to feel the crushing disappointment that conversations about sex and mating and changing always brought on. The sense of failure. My hands in my hair, I tugged and bit back the tears burning my eyes. Someday, she'd trust me. Someday, she'd hear me.

Someday, she'd love me enough to want to keep me forever.

FIVE

Angelita

I RACED THROUGH THE woods, following the coast of the little island the local Feral Breed called their own. The supernatural population of the place had been growing for a couple for years at that point, creating an almost private reserve for themselves. The guys had bought as much land as they could, making sure property lines butted up against one another and stretched from the water inland. Each lot differed in size and shape, each house unique, but the overall sense of the place was one of wilderness and privacy. There were acres to run on and huge plots of land where no outsiders ever seemed to come. A shifter and witch sanctuary surrounded by nature. I liked it. I liked it even more that Julian lived there. What I didn't like was crossing paths with other shifters while out.

I ran the length of the properties, trying to clear my head. Needing to shake off the dread I'd felt after my conversation with Julian the night before. We'd gone to bed together, even cuddled like we normally loved to do, but I hadn't been able to sleep. So I'd crawled out of bed at the ass crack of dawn and headed into the woods. I wanted to be alone to think, but that wasn't an option, apparently. Before I'd even reached the first property line of the forest, two wolves appeared from the dappled shadows under the trees. Two I recognized well. Rebel and Bez ran with me, one on each flank. Following me down the path and through the trees. Keeping pace with me but not coming too close. Guarding me. Their positions didn't help calm me a bit. I didn't like people trying to sneak up on me, and my wolf didn't like to be followed. Luckily, we both liked to compete.

As we circled around at the shore and began the trek back through the forest, I picked up the pace, pumping my legs faster, harder. I'd taken this from a leisurely run to a race, and there was no way I'd lose. My wolf wouldn't allow it.

I growled as I passed over a trail through the middle of the property, one leading from Phoenix's cabin to Beast's. I didn't turn, though. I kept running south, heading for Rebel's home. For Julian. The man who probably didn't want to talk to me after last night.

Why did things have to be so complicated? We'd struggled since meeting just to be able to spend time together, and now that we were old enough to demand freedom, we couldn't find a middle ground on what the future should be. I wanted to exchange mating bites, but he wanted more than that. To be like me. And as much as I would have loved that, would have been completely blissful running in the woods with my wolf mate by my side, the idea of him being turned—of killing his human side and giving him an inner wolf to share his body—terrified me. Some humans made it through just fine—Rebel himself had been born human. Others…they lost memories, like Phoenix had. For years after his turning, he couldn't remember his own surname. I knew of Anbizens who'd damn near lost their minds, becoming hardened and crazed. Thirsty for blood. I couldn't let that happen to my sweet Julian. I wouldn't. But how to stop him from pursuing something so dangerous?

Too lost in my thoughts to pay attention to my footing, I scrambled across the gravel as I came onto Rebel's property, following the driveway toward the garage. The two wolves ran in right after me, breathing hard, snappish with each other as they battled for second place. Typical males.

As soon as I rushed through the open garage door, I shifted human, smirking to cover my heavy heart, and grabbed one of the cloaks Rebel kept on the workbench at the back. Being around humans meant covering up our nakedness as often as possible, something still slightly foreign to me, having grown up in a pack. Nudity and shifters went together. It was a simple fact of life. One I was still learning to ignore.

"Fight all you want, boys. Second place is really just the first loser."

"You'd fit with my clan well. They all fight to win."

I spun, crouching and growling as I faced the stranger in the shadows. But as he stepped forward, the fact that he wasn't truly a stranger caught me off guard. The bear shifter had come back.

"What do you want?" My heart jumped, but not in fear. No, I wasn't afraid. I was excited. He came back, which meant he was desperate. No shifter would ignore the order of an alpha wolf on his own turf. Not without damn good reason. Wolves were territorial and dangerous when threatened, especially ones as strong as Rebel. This boded well for me, but I'd need to get the bear away from the others. Somehow.

"What the fuck are you doing here?" Rebel asked as soon as he shifted human, his voice pure warning.

One the bear chose to ignore. "I came to try my luck one more time."

"I told you. We're not—"

"I know." Bear-man put his hands up, his eyes darting my way a few too many times to be casual. "It's not normally what you do, but we're desperate. My clan needs that statue."

A chill went up my spine. Desperate…just as I'd expected. This was it. My chance. But how…

Bez slipped closer to me, guarding as always and silent as a snake. "The man said no already and asked you to leave his property."

The bear's eyes seemed to glow with something close to anger. Irritation, maybe? Frustration? "Yes, I remember."

"Then perhaps you'd better take his dir—"

"What does the idol do?" I asked, too caught up in the gold of the bear shifter's eyes to ignore him. How did humans think that was normal?

Those weird, yellow eyes turned my way. Focusing hard. Devouring me in a single look. "It's a fertility goddess."

"Oh." I crept past Bez, ignoring his low growl as I moved out of his range. "And why do you need it so badly?"

The bear raised his arm to straighten his collar, and I flinched. Ready to run away. It wasn't often another shifter could make me feel like prey, but this one did. His bear outweighed my wolf for sure, my size almost a joke in comparison to his. But there was something else about him. Something dangerous and deadly. Something that made me more cautious around him.

His head cocked, his eyes completely locked on me still. "Without the idol, we can't complete our matings. Our pairs end up in a limbo the fates never intended for them."

Sounded a lot like Julian and me. "That sucks."

"Yes, it does," he said, a slight smile tugging on one side of his mouth. "Especially when you consider that we can't breed without being mated."

Rebel's angry face fell, and even Bez seemed concerned as he asked, "How long since you've had it?"

"Sixty-five years next week."

"Holy fuck." And here I'd been complaining about the few years Julian and I'd had to wait. Sixty-five? That sounded tortuous.

"Yeah, that about sums it up." Bear leaned against the workbench, crossing his legs at the ankles. "Sixty-five years of a cubless clan. It took us decades to figure out where the damned thing was, and now that we know, we need to get it back. None of my clan is skilled in such delicate matters, though. So you can understand my desperation to find someone to assist me in my retrieval."

"I can," Rebel said. "But it's not what my guys do."

I caught Bez's eye, matching his raised eyebrow. That job sounded like something *his guys*, the Dire Wolves, would do. Why he wasn't jumping in to help, I had no idea.

"I don't like your answer, wolf, but I understand it." The bear sighed again and pushed off the workbench, making the whole thing creak under the strain. "I'm staying at the Grand Hotel if you change your mind."

Rebel nodded once. "I won't, but if I hear of anyone who can help you, I'll send them your way."

"Much appreciated." His gold eyes met mine once more, and his lips twisted into a smile that made me want to recoil. "Be safe, little wolf. And take good care of that baby I heard crying the other day."

Before Rebel could rip the man's throat out for bringing up his son, I jumped in with, "It's not mine."

The bear only shrugged. "It takes a clan to raise a cub. Not that we'd know much about that anymore."

He left with little fanfare, trudging down the driveway toward a minivan that definitely didn't scream dangerous predator or paranormal phenomenon. What a way to blend in.

"Why won't you help him?" I asked Bez as soon as the bear had driven off.

"He's not one of us."

"So?"

"So, bears can't be trusted."

"Neither can wolves."

He twisted his lips into a deadly smile, probably knowing I was simply repeating back what he'd told me a million times over the years. "True, but I can kill a wolf easily enough."

"You've killed werewolves and vampires. I'm pretty sure you could kill a bear."

"I'm sure, too. But I don't want to have to, so I avoid them."

The men followed me to the porch. Dawn had barely broken, and the humans were sleeping. I could hear Sariel in the house, probably in the kitchen preparing something for breakfast as she waited for little Elijah to rise. She loved that baby, loved taking care of him and doting on him. She'd been the same way with me when I came to live with her. She was a natural mother, one who couldn't have children of her own.

Just like those bear shifters.

"So," Rebel said as he settled on a chair against the railing, pulling me from my heartbreaking thoughts. I curled up in the corner of the porch swing, watching him, as Bez leaned on the railing. "What's the plan?"

"What plan?" I asked.

"The plan for turning Julian."

And there went any thoughts of babies or bears. "I won't."

Rebel's eyebrows dropped, furrowing in what appeared to be confusion. "Why the hell not?"

"Uh, because it's dangerous? Because the transition could drive him mad? Because I could lose him?"

Rebel sat back, dismissing me with nothing more than a frown. "You won't lose him."

"How do you know?"

"Because Julian not making it through would kill my mate, and that's not about to happen. I have to put my trust in the fates to pull him through the turning."

I pulled my legs underneath me, shaking my head. "What if I can't do it?"

"Then I will." Bez met my eyes, his hard and sure. "I'm stronger and more wolf than most because of my Dire lineage. I'll be his wolf giver if you won't."

I shook my head. "No."

"He wants this," Rebel said. "And I want the two of you to have a long, happy life together."

"We can do that as mates, without turning him."

"No, you can't," Bez said. "Not if he wants more than that."

Rebel nodded. "He'd do anything for you. Why won't you do the same for him?"

I stared, shocked. I loved Julian…how could they possibly doubt that?

"What if he dies?" I finally asked, my voice weak even to my own ears. My biggest fear laid out before them.

"He won't," Bez answered, so solid and sure.

"But how do you *know* that?"

He tilted his head, his eyes swirling a bit from blue to silver as only the Dire Wolves could do. "You have to trust, Angelita. Trust in the fates, in yourself, and in your Omega wolf. You are more powerful than you think."

I stood, itching to run again. Wanting to escape from the conversation. From the possibility of losing Julian. "Yeah, well, trust doesn't come easy."

Sariel opened the door then, looking me over quickly before smiling my way. "Angelita? Breakfast will be ready soon. Do you want to go grab Julian?"

"Sure." I thought I caught a ghost of sadness on her face as she turned away, but I didn't take the time to examine that. I wanted my mate and was beyond ready to be done with the two meddling father figures. What the hell did they know? They'd never lost their family. They'd never been safe and warm one minute, then afraid they wouldn't survive the next. They had no idea how hard this would be on me if I messed up. If I lost Julian.

I could *not* lose him.

I rushed up the stairs, my heart aching for my mate as my emotions roiled inside of me. I had to see him, needed to touch him, to know he was safe. Hell, I craved the very sight of him. My wolf wouldn't settle until I was able to feel that he was whole and healthy still. Irrational, maybe. Excessive, absolutely. Stoppable, not in the least.

The stairs were no match for my speed. The door sat unlocked, the room still dark beyond it. I didn't even pause in my quest, though. My eyes adjusted to the lack of light before the door had swung closed. *Julian.* He lay sprawled across the bed, hugging my pillow in a way that made my heart trip. My mate slept peacefully, all blissfully rumpled and relaxed. An irresistible sight.

I stalked across the floor as quietly as I could, not wanting to disturb him. Yet. My wolf whined in my head with every step. She wanted our mate too. Wanted to sniff and touch and rub up against. She wanted contact, physicality, something tactile to prove he was okay. But most of all, she wanted to claim him as ours. A fact that made my body shake with the fight to restrain her.

As I reached the bed, I dropped my cloak. This was my mate, my Julian. The only man I'd ever wanted and would ever want. I didn't need to cover myself around him. I slipped under the covers and pressed my body to his, sighing as the warmth of his skin seeped into mine.

He was safe.

"Good morning," he mumbled as his hands began to trail lazily over my bare back. I pressed my ear to his chest, relishing every thump of his heart, every rise as he breathed. Safe, safe, safe. And so very mine,

We lay like that for a while, Julian stroking my back, me

draped across his chest. The way the sunlight peeked behind the blinds brought a golden glow to the edges of the room, the quiet of a morning in the woods blanketing us. I could have stayed like that for days. Weeks, even. But not Julian.

"You smell like the forest," he said, sounding far more awake than I wanted him to be. "You've been running?"

"Yeah. Rebel and Bez joined me."

"That must have been fun." His sarcasm didn't escape my notice.

"Not. But I won the race back, so it was worthwhile."

I bit back anything about the bear shifter. It made no sense, really. I told Julian everything. But not this time. I needed to plan a little more, to have a solid path going forward for us. I needed to keep my cards close to the vest before I dragged Julian into anything.

And that need to protect, to keep something from my mate, was a far better wake-up call than anything could be.

"C'mon," I said as I untangled myself from Julian's hold. "Sariel said breakfast would be ready soon."

He didn't move, though. Didn't roll away or make an attempt to get up. "Everything okay?"

No, not right now. "Of course. I'm just hungry."

"Okay." He rolled off the bed, heading for me the second his feet hit the floor. He wrapped his arms around me from behind, enveloping me in his scent and warmth once more. I sank back, melting against him. Letting the feel of his skin be my anchor.

"I love you, Juls."

"I love you too, Leelee." He nuzzled into my neck, kissing the length of it before he rubbed his lips against my ear and whispered, "I'll let you hide from me right now because it feels like you need to, but we'll talk about it later. Now, let's get dressed so we can join the family for breakfast."

Squeezing my eyes closed, I nodded. Later. I needed to think up a plan to find the bear shifter later. I needed to…do something. I just wasn't sure what yet.

SIX

Julian

THERE SHOULD HAVE BEEN something soothing about sitting on the couch in Charlotte and Rebel's house. Something familiar. I'd taken up that particular post since the day my sister and I had packed our stuff and moved in with the guy. Wolf. Whatever. I'd sat in that exact spot while they talked about their days, while they planned their futures, and while they argued. And man, could they argue. Sometimes Rebel's eighteenth-century ideals clashed hard with my sister's twenty-first-century ones. Still, they worked things out and stayed together, building a team of two that could weather anything life threw at them, it seemed. And they'd always included me in their discussions and plans.

I'd sat in my spot when they told me Elijah was coming—a nephew that I would never see but would still love with all my heart. I'd sat in that spot when they'd told me about mates and claimings and what my bond with Angelita meant. And in the last couple of years, Angelita had sat right at my side as my family and hers grew more entwined because of us. I'd sat in that spot through some of the biggest moments of my life.

So I should have been comfortable and at peace. Instead,

I bounced my leg and picked at what felt like a ridge of fabric under my arm. I couldn't sit still. Something was up with Angelita. She'd been distracted for days, ever since the morning run she'd taken with Rebel and Bez. Not just distracted… distant. Not physically. No, that aspect of our relationship was as strong as ever. The more emotional stuff was there, too. But the rest…the talking. The attention. The feeling that I knew everything about her…gone. Something was wrong.

"Where's Angelita?" Charlotte asked. Elijah squeaked and squealed, which meant he was about to be fed. The kid seemed happiest when he got to eat. Hell, he was just plain happy most of the time. Me…not so much.

"She went to the city with Bez. Something about a used bookstore she wanted to visit." *Distance.*

"I'm surprised you didn't go with her."

I grunted, avoiding that topic. I'd wanted to go, was more than willing to stumble around after her. But she'd wanted to spend time with Bez. Another thing that didn't sit well with me—she never wanted to spend time alone with Bez when she visited me. Not that I blamed her or would have gotten in the way—he was the closest thing she had to a father these days. No, it wasn't that I wanted to stop them. It was more that she seemed determined to get away from me this morning, and that fact had been eating at me for hours.

"Do you ever—" I froze, unable to say the words. Or unwilling.

But my sister wasn't really one to let people get away with hiding. "Do I ever what? Need space from Rebel?"

It was irritating how smart she was. "No. Do you ever feel left behind by him because you're not…like him?"

She went silent. Elijah gurgled and made smacking noises as he ate whatever she was feeding him. The wind whistled past the windows, and the sound of a dog barking somewhere too far away to worry about punctuated the otherwise still house. Too still. Too empty, as well.

"You want her to change you into one of them," Charlotte said. Not asking.

I nodded, wishing for the first time in a while that I could actually see her face. That I could gauge her reaction with my own eyes.

"Are you sure you want that commitment?"

There was only one answer. "Yes. I'm not worried about my commitment to her. I love her, she's my mate. That's not the issue."

"So then, what is the issue?"

"She doesn't want to turn me."

Charlotte hummed. "She's afraid of losing you."

"Yeah."

"You understand why, right?"

"Of course." And I did. It was something we'd talked about a hundred times—her losing her family and me losing most of mine. "But I'm more fragile as a human."

"Except during the turning."

"I'll make it through."

"And if you don't?"

Her simple question pulled me up short.

"Julian, not all humans have the strength to live through that, or they finish the turning and their minds and personalities have completely disintegrated." She made a cooing noise and something rattled, which probably meant Elijah was done eating and she was setting him up for playtime on the floor.

"Bring him to me," I said, craving a distraction. Elijah's warm weight landed on my lap a few seconds later, and his sweet baby smell filled my senses. "Hey, buddy. Did you have a good snack?"

"He did," Charlotte answered for him as she moved away

from me. Probably heading to the chair closest to the windows. If this was my spot, that was hers. "He's a good eater. Reminds me of you when you were little."

"You always say that."

"And I always mean it." She grew quiet again as Elijah grabbed hold of my face and pulled me closer.

I kissed his nose, smiling when he giggled. "She's going to remember every little thing about you, kid."

"Just like I do with you," Charlotte said. "And just like Angelita will as well."

"She's my mate, not my family."

"Yes, but she loves you. My memories come from that place—both the good ones and the bad ones."

"Char—"

"Do you know how hard it was to watch you suffer?"

I couldn't answer her, a fact she seemed to understand because she certainly didn't stop.

"I'd just lost Mom and Dad, and I was so relieved that I at least got to keep you. But then the doctors started trying to explain what was going on and what you'd lost. You nearly died twice while I watched."

"But I didn't."

"Right. But you're not the same boy I knew. You never will be." She sighed. "Julian, you are so strong. Fiercely independent and smart in ways that eclipse me. But there are still times when I miss pieces of you that we lost that day."

"My sight."

"No, not that. You've never let your blindness get in your way. More your easy laugh and carefree attitude. You were so confident and free before the accident, but afterward, a lot of that disappeared."

"And you think that's why she's reluctant? She's afraid I'll change enough for her to…lose me?"

"What do you think?" Her footsteps moved closer, and Elijah squealed as she lifted him from my lap.

"I think she's afraid, but I'm not sure why."

"Men are clueless, Elijah," she said in a singsong voice. "She's not just afraid of losing you from her life entirely. She's afraid of losing bits of you that she loves. Bits that love her just as fiercely. If you knew something would change her personality and possibly make her not care about you anymore, would you want that?"

Easy answer. "No."

"So?"

"So I need to try to understand where she's coming from and stop pushing her." I hated when she was so right.

"Sounds smart to me."

But as Charlotte walked away with Elijah, I still didn't feel as if I'd solved anything. Angelita's reasons for not changing me were clear enough. It was her reasons for pulling away over the last few days that were bothering me so much. Where was she, and why didn't she want me to go with her? My mate was focusing on something that she wouldn't share with me, and that was definitely not the norm.

I needed to get her to talk to me.

SEVEN

Angelita

THE USED BOOKSTORE LOOMED over the other buildings on the block. While the building wasn't particularly large, the height of it made up for its slim width in spades. White brick—painted too many times to see the indentations of the mortar—flaked around the single front window, and the recessed door appeared almost more menacing than welcoming. But above all that, the windows continued for many, many floors. Rows of dark, dirty glass stacked one on top of another and another and another, indicating numerous floors of bookshelves, dark corners, and places to get lost.

It looked like the perfect spot for what I needed to do.

"This is where you want to go?" Bez stared up at the building, a frown marring his already harsh face.

"Yeah. Supposedly, they have a killer antique book collection on the upper floors. I'm in the mood to dig."

"Hunting books." Bez huffed. "Okay, then, let's go inside."

I walked ahead of him, scoping out the dark first floor. Stacks upon stacks of books sat anywhere they could—on shelves, on top of cases, on chairs. The piles seemed endless and haphazard. Bez tried to look uninterested, but his natural curiosity quickly got the better of him. He ran a finger over one stack of books, then the length of a shelf, and when he picked up a battered old volume with some foreign language embossed in gold on the side, I knew I had him.

"I'm going to head up to the fantasy section." I edged toward the stairs, crossing my fingers that he didn't follow me. At least not yet.

Bez snorted, raising an eyebrow as he gave me a quick glance. "Yeah. You do that. See if anything sounds familiar."

With a laugh, I turned and rushed up the dark and dusty staircase. Six flights up, and I was stalking across the old wooden floor, looking for options. On the far side, a window opened up to a view of the neighborhood around the store. That was my objective…my goal. Without pausing, I popped the window open and slid out. The two-story drop to the roof of the building attached to the side of the bookstore wasn't anything I couldn't handle, and within seconds, I was on the sidewalk and rushing down the block. If I had my plan worked out right, I had about fifty minutes before Bez would really start looking for me. He was a book hound—a total nut when it came to old maps and travel journals. The used bookstore would be like crack for him, but that draw wouldn't last forever. Not with how protective he could be. I needed to haul ass.

The Grand Hotel sat on a rather unimpressive stretch of what was probably once a decent Main Street. The character of the building, the charm of the brick walls and low-slung porch, made up for the drab location. I hurried inside their dark wood double doors and across the foyer, letting my senses take over. The scent of bear lingered in corners and hallways, but I could tell the man I was after wasn't there. The smell felt too old, too faded. No, he wasn't around. Not on the first floor, at least.

I headed for the stairs, rushing up them on a mission, trying hard not to let my wolf out too much. I needed my senses, but there were a lot of humans around. I had to at least appear to be one of them, which meant reining in the beast within even when she wanted to hunt as much as I needed her to.

On the third-floor landing, the heavy scent of bear nearly knocked me over. This. The man had to be here somewhere. And by the stench of the big beasts, he wasn't alone. I hadn't considered that in my plans. Still, he needed something I had the skills to get, and I needed something he had the resources to provide. Easy trade.

I hoped.

Before I took even three steps down the hall, a door opened at the far end, and the man I'd been coming to see stepped out. A woman quickly followed him, but she wasn't my concern. I hoped it would stay that way.

Show time. "Yo. Bear."

The man's head shot up, those golden eyes of his locking on mine. Recognition flashed across his face for just a second before rage replaced it.

"Get back in the room," he muttered. The woman, a tall, strawberry-blond sculpture of curves and femininity gave me one hell of a glare before slipping back inside and shutting the door. I waited, knowing the bear would defend himself and his—Mate? Friend? Family?—if I dared take a single step closer. Hell, any wolf would have as well. But I couldn't care about her right then—I had business to do. With the red-haired, bearded man who could probably squash me without breaking a sweat. He'd have to catch me first, though.

He stalked closer, keeping his eyes on mine. Keeping his face hard with fury. If the growl behind his words was any indication, I'd truly pissed him off. "I can't say I was expecting to see you, little wolf."

"Yeah, well. I like to keep people on their toes."

"Where are your guard dogs?"

"At home in the kennel."

A smile almost broke through that chiseled face. One that looked a lot more wicked than happy. "You came here alone? Do you really think that's wise?"

I shrugged, leaning against the wall as if I didn't have a care in the world. As if my wolf wasn't snarling and foaming at the mouth with every step closer he took. "You won't hurt me."

"How can you be so sure?"

Here we go. "Because I can get you what you want."

He tried hard to stay stoic, but a tic in his jaw gave him away. He was interested. "And what might that be?"

"Money first."

He blinked. "Excuse me?"

"You told Rebel you'd give him anything to get the idol back."

"Yes."

It was my turn to stalk closer, to approach. To show a little wolf aggression. "I want money."

"I don't have times for games, little wolf." He turned as if to leave me in the hall, something I'd been ready for.

"Money for an idol," I said, keeping my voice loud and strong. "A mate for a mate."

He spun, growling. "What are you talking about?"

"You need the statue so you can claim your mate fully, have lots of little cubs, and get your happily ever after." I stepped closer, keeping my eyes on his. Refusing to yield. "I need money so I can stay with my mate, have a few pups, and get *my* happily ever after."

He didn't respond, but he didn't leave either. I took that as a good sign, so I kept going.

"A rogue band of wolves murdered my family. My guardians want to keep me safe, but their idea of safe is locked away on a ranch in Texas. My mate is here, and he's human. He deserves to do all those human things like go to college, but he won't because it will keep us apart. I need money. If I can support us, he can do what he wants, and we can still stay together and be independent."

The bear stood stock-still, his glare changing to a look of contemplation. "You need money to claim your mate."

"Yes, and you need that idol to claim yours."

"The idol is in the Federal Bank building on Biddle. Eight stories of alarms and cameras and motion detectors. You think you can get into that building, kid?"

Jackpot. "I know I can."

He sneered, taking a good look at me from the tip of my toes to the top of my head. Assessing. "You don't look much like a thief."

Thinking quickly, wanting to spin my plans in a positive light, I came back with, "I'm not a thief—I'm a bounty hunter."

"*You're* a bounty hunter?"

"Yeah. You give me a bounty to find, and I hunt it. So what do you say—do you need the services of Feral Breed Bounty Hunting or not?"

He sighed, looking at me with a wariness I couldn't really fault. "How do I know I'll get what I'm paying for?"

"You tell me what I'm hunting, and I'll retrieve it. No money until I deliver the goods."

"Not even a deposit?"

"I trust your word."

"You shouldn't."

I inched even closer, still not backing down. Desperate in a way I'd never been before. "Do we have a deal?"

He didn't look convinced. "Why do I feel as if I'm going to regret this?"

My grin was unstoppable. I handed him a slip of paper I'd carried from home. "Here's my email. Send me everything you can on the idol—where it is, who has it, what it looks like. Anything at all. I'll be in touch."

I was halfway down the hall and headed for the stairs when he hollered, "You're just going to leave?"

"My guard is waiting for me at the bookstore. I can't ditch him for the whole day. He'll get suspicious."

"I don't even know your name."

Ooh, yeah. Probably shouldn't let him know my real one. I hadn't thought about that, but I was nothing if not creative. I grabbed the newel post, looking over my shoulder one last time. "Just call me Angel."

Five blocks, one slightly off-putting climb up a rusted-out gutter, and a quick trip to the ladies' room to wash off any possibility of bear scent, and I was headed down the stairs at the bookstore. With every step, I had to remind myself to stay calm, keep it together, don't give off any signs that I'd just enacted a plan to steal back an idol from an armed building for a bear shifter we knew basically nothing about. No big deal. Average Tuesday.

I was never going to pull this off.

I found Bez on the second floor, resting against a wall in the corner, a thick, black tome in his hands. He looked engrossed, casual, completely unaware that I'd left the building. Mission accomplished…so far.

"Find anything good?" I fought to keep my voice light and my breathing steady.

Bez glanced up, his swirling silver eyes focusing on mine. "These humans have their history all wrong."

So far, so good. "Yeah, that tends to happen."

He snorted and tossed the book on a windowsill. "Are you ready to go?"

I lifted one shoulder in a lazy sort of shrug. "Sure."

"You're not buying any books."

"I didn't really see anything that caught my eye."

As expected, Bez didn't argue. He simply followed me out of the store, shadowing me all the way to the truck he'd borrowed from Rebel.

"Where to?" he asked once we'd climbed inside.

"Home." I glanced out the mirror, running my fingertip over the glass as we drove past the Grand Hotel. Excitement and hope making my heart pound a little harder. A little faster. My final escape was at hand, the only thing standing between me and freedom an alarm system I needed to skirt. And a mate I still hadn't told my plans to.

"Want me to drive through that coffee place you like?"

I shook my head, guilt heavy in my heart. "I need to see Julian."

EIGHT

Julian

I FELT ANGELITA DRAWING closer long before I heard the car turning off the main road into our little enclave of shifters, humans, and witches. A pulse started in my chest, a thrumming that only happened when she was near. Something that replaced the empty feeling I lived with when we were apart.

I stood from my chair and moved toward the door the second tires hit our driveway, almost shaking in anticipation. I needed her—wanted to know she had come back to me, craved our connection to be reinforced.

"Is that them?" Sariel called, her footsteps bringing her closer to the door. And me. I couldn't answer her, didn't care to. She had wolf senses—she knew her mate was back along with mine.

The car stopped, and the driver cut the engine. Just another few seconds, and Angelita would be in my arms.

"Hey, babe," Bez called. Two doors slammed shut, two sets of footsteps grew louder as they neared. Why wasn't she saying anything?

"Hey," Sariel replied, sounding way too happy. "You two are just in time. We were about to put dinner on the table."

"Perfect. I'm starving. Hey, Julian," Bez said as he passed me. There were the soft sounds of the two coming together, probably a hug or a kiss. Nothing I had time to worry about. I stood and waited for my mate, for my turn. A greeting, a hug, a kiss…something from my Angelita on her return. Anything at all to calm the rush of need swamping me.

When Sariel and Bez retreated to the kitchen, I finally got what I'd been waiting for. Angelita's little hand slid into mine, tentative and slow. Fuck that. I yanked her closer and wrapped her in my arms, sighing when she grabbed my neck and buried her head against my chest. We'd spent months apart at a time over the years. Why had these last few hours been so difficult? Why was I so needy for her all of a sudden?

I held her tighter, nearly pulling her off the floor as I buried my face in her neck and breathed her in. Safe. Back. Mine.

"Julian," Angelita whispered, her breath warm against my chest. Her body practically vibrating in my arms.

"Leelee." I could have held her forever. Could have picked her up and carried her back to my apartment right then. I needed her that much.

But she pushed away far too soon, pulling her warmth from me. "We should get inside. Dinner's ready."

I nodded, clinging to her hand. Unable to let her go. "Where were you? I woke up, and Sariel said you'd left with Bez."

"We went to the mainland."

That sounded…vague. "For what?"

Her arm pulled, the sign that she had shrugged. A move she only did when she was trying to hide something. Angelita wasn't a shrugger, and the fact that she'd just done that to me, knowing I'd catch the tell for what it was, nearly floored me.

"We went to a bookstore."

And that was the first time I ever knew Angelita to flat out lie to me. Dropping her hand, I turned and walked into the house without another word, something hot and sharp piercing my chest. Something that felt too much like betrayal.

"Oh, Julian and Angelita. Perfect." Charlotte grabbed my arm, oblivious to the rage and hurt swirling inside of me. "I was about to come looking for you two. Why don't you go ahead and sit down? Everything's ready."

I took my usual seat, Angelita sliding into the chair beside me beside me. Normal. Except that I didn't reach for her hand or tug her chair closer. No, I sat stiff and still, wishing this could all be over so I could retreat to my room and try to figure out what the fuck had just happened. But I had family dinner to deal with, so I ignored the elephant in the room…and my mate. A fact that seemed to make her nervous if the sound of her leg shaking was any indication.

Dinner dragged, awkward and completely unusual for us. I chose not to participate in the conversation and Angelita barely spoke at all as well, so long silences plagued the meal. I didn't eat much either, something my sister definitely noticed.

"Are you feeling okay?" Charlotte grabbed my arm as I stood to leave the table, her voice much more concerned than I cared to hear.

So I pasted on my best smile and squeezed her hand. "Yeah. Just tired."

Though, my sister was nothing if not observant. "If you're sure that's all."

I was halfway to the door when Angelita spoke up.

"I'd like to be excused as well. I'll take Julian back to his apartment so he can rest."

"Thanks, Angelita," Rebel said. I waited for Angelita to come, for her to hold out her elbow for me to grab even though I didn't need it. At that moment, I didn't want it, but I couldn't refuse her. Then everyone would know something was wrong, and I wanted to keep at least some of our business private.

Things like how I needed to make sure she knew that lying to me wasn't an option.

Once we were outside and far enough away that even Rebel wouldn't hear us, I pounced. "Want to tell me where you really went today?"

"I told you—a bookstore."

"You're lying."

"No, I really went to a bookstore."

"Fine. Where else did you go?"

"Julian, I don't—"

"Don't want to tell me the truth?"

"No, I don't want to drag you into something that may turn out to be a stupid idea."

"I love your stupid ideas."

"Julian." She sounded irritated. Good.

"I love you, Leelee. Never doubt that." I pulled her to a stop at the bottom of the stairs leading to my apartment. "But I won't accept you lying to me."

"Please," she whispered, inching closer. "Just give me a couple of days to see if this pans out. I don't want to get your hopes up."

I sighed and took to the stairs. "Tell me."

"I can't."

"We don't keep secrets from each other, Angelita."

If my calling her by her full name stung at all, she didn't let that hurt affect her path. "It's just for a few days."

I threw open my door and stormed inside, pacing in a way I hadn't done in years. For the first time since a little wolf brushed against my legs during one of the darker days of my life, I felt something for Angelita that wasn't positive. I felt…anger. And I didn't know how to deal with that.

"Fine. You need a few days, but I won't like it." I grabbed my pillow off the bed and headed for the couch. Well, love seat, which wouldn't work for my height. Fuck. I couldn't tear the too-small piece of furniture apart, so instead, I snagged the blankets off the bed and laid everything down on the soft rug my sister had demanded I put down when I'd moved into the place. Thank you, Charlotte.

"What are you doing?" Angelita asked from somewhere by the door.

"Just like I said at dinner—I'm tired."

"But your bed—"

"You sleep in it."

Silence. Tension. And when she did finally speak, her voice sounded absolutely pained. "You're not going to join me?"

"No, Angelita. I'm not. I love you, but I don't like being lied to. When you're ready to be honest with me, then we can talk. Until that time, I'd rather sleep on the floor and listen to the television than cuddle."

I pressed the power button on my remote and switched the channel to where I knew national news played all the time. The negativity was the perfect accompaniment to my mood. I closed my eyes and listened to the voices, not wanting to speak another word to my mate. My heart ached every moment to fix whatever had gone wrong, but it wasn't my place to do so. It was hers. And she… Well, she wasn't budging.

I fell asleep in front of the television. Woke up in the middle of the night there too, but with the apartment quiet, the television silent, and a warm body cuddled against mine. Angelita. She'd joined me on the floor, covering both of us with the comforter from the bed. Her even breathing and slow heart rate were signs she was in deep sleep. On the goddamned floor. I may have been upset with her, but I wasn't an asshole.

I pulled the comforter off us and tossed it on the foot of the bed. Once I had my bearings, I picked up Angelita and carried her to the bed. She grunted and sighed, but otherwise slept on. Good. We didn't need to fight again. I set her down on the mattress, covering her with the comforter and sitting on the edge. Fuck, I hated this. I missed her already. Missed our closeness and our connection. How would I survive a few days of her keeping things from me at this rate?

Truth was, I wouldn't. So I needed to choose…give her the time she needed for whatever plan she'd concocted, or cut myself off from her and try to force her to tell me?

Okay, maybe I was an asshole. At least, I had been.

Surrendering to my need for contact, I crawled under the comforter with her. She immediately curled into my side, wrapping her little body around mine and holding on tightly. As if I'd leave her. As if there was any way I could.

"Oh, Leelee. Why can't things ever be easy?" I kissed the top of her head, then pulled her closer. Fuck being mad for a little while. There would be time for that in the morning.

But even as sleep reclaimed me, even as Angelita's heart pounded in time with mine, the fear grew inside of me. She'd lied, and that was something we needed to deal with if we were going to move forward in our relationship.

Something that could never happen again.

NINE

Angelita

JULIAN WAS MAD.

Not fighting mad, or screaming mad—that broody sort of mad that kept me on edge all through the next day. He wasn't rude or dismissive—in fact, from the outside, it probably looked as if everything was fine.

But he wasn't touching me.

Such a little thing, touch. The brush of someone's skin against yours, the warmth of one body against another. When we were living so far apart, I'd missed his touch often. Had craved it with an obsession bordering on painful. This was worse. He sat right there next to me, close enough to see, to smell, to sense. And yet…nothing.

Just a few more days had become my mantra. I needed to do this job without any help from the Feral Breed or the Dire Wolves if I was going to prove myself to them all. One job, one wolf…that would signal success. Sadly, that meant keeping Julian in the dark. If he knew, he'd worry. If he worried, he might do something stupid like try to help me, which would put him in the sights of bear shifters and possibly other paranormals. My human mate couldn't stand against them—he wouldn't have a chance. And I refused to risk him for what was still just the possibility of a career.

Only a few more days.

"Heading up for the night?"

I jumped at Charlotte's voice. She watched Julian, who was already halfway through the doorway into the kitchen. I hadn't even noticed he'd gotten up.

"Yeah." Julian paused, almost seeming to look in my direction. "I'm not feeling all that great."

"Oh, okay. Maybe it's best if you go. We don't want Elijah to get sick." She adjusted the smiling baby on her hip, almost seeming to pull him farther away from Julian.

"That's what I figured." He hesitated. Waiting for something, it seemed. But not for long. Not long enough for me to figure out what to do. "Good night."

And then he was gone, leaving me behind. That had never happened before, and yet, it actually worked in my favor. I had preplanning to do, which would require me to sneak away from him. As much as it had hurt, his walking away from me gave me the window I needed. It was time to go to work.

"You're not tired?" Charlotte asked as she took a seat across from me. Elijah clapped and blew spit bubbles, obviously wanting to play. Not what I needed.

"No, I'm not tired." I rose and headed for the door. "I think I'll go for a run."

"The guys are at the denhouse. Do you want me to call around and find someone to go with you?"

Of course, Rebel, Sariel, and Bez were hanging out at the Feral Breed denhouse downtown. Having them off island definitely helped my situation. Knowing I'd lied to Julian didn't.

Just a few more days.

I shrugged, fighting to stay casual. "Nah, I don't need a babysitter. I won't go off property."

"Okay, then," she said, distracted by Elijah's reaching and pulling. "Be careful out there."

"I will. Don't wait up—I'll just head up to Julian's when I get back." And then I was gone. I grabbed the bag I'd hidden in the bushes and raced up the driveway until I found the path all the local wolves used. Tucked into the trees, I quickly stripped, stored my clothes, and shifted wolf. Time to use four paws to move and my teeth to hold my stuff.

It took me twice as long running instead of driving to get to the office building I was looking for because I had to slink and backtrack to avoid humans, but that wasn't too bad. At least I knew I could reach my destination without needing any sort of vehicle. Now if I could just complete the task without requiring help. Then everything could go back to normal—or rather, the new normal. Julian and I could live together, independent of our guardians. The freedom was so close, I could practically smell it. My plans had to work.

A few more days. One job. A chance to start a business that could support us and allow him to go back to school while I took care of the money. He was the only thing keeping me moving forward, the only person I truly needed in my life. The last twenty-four hours with him so upset at me had been hellish, but we'd been through worse. This too would pass. I just had to finish this job.

In the alley behind the Federal Bank building, I found a deep pit of shadows and shifted human. Once I pulled my clothes on, I tied my hair back, tucked the bag I'd brought under a dumpster for safekeeping, and headed for the fire escape. Of the building next door.

The bear—whom I'd begun calling Red in my thoughts— had emailed me everything he knew about the location of the idol along with pictures and size. I'd studied building plans, permit histories, and rental agreements for hours, learning everything I could about the place I needed to access. Including that the easiest way in would actually be from the top.

See, the Federal Bank building still had an actual bank on the bottom floor. The rest of the floors? All broken up into office rentals. The lower floors had the tightest security, so to the roof I would go. But the Federal Bank building didn't have accessible fire escapes. The building next door did.

Up the rickety stairs, across the flat roof, and over to the edge joining the building I really wanted into, I moved with stealth. Keeping to the shadows. Slipping across the littered roof to get to the HVAC units. Both buildings had similar setups—tall, silver boxes with vents hanging off one side. Both vents pointed toward the shared alley between them. That left me about an eight-foot gap from one building to the next. An easy jump for a wolf shifter for sure. No problem.

"You got this," I whispered as I found my balance on top of the first unit. I hadn't expected the metal to be so slippery, but I could deal with that. I pulled off my shoes and tossed them across the divide, bending my toes to cup my feet against the metal. Ready.

With a deep breath, I let my wolf push forward enough for her strength to infuse my muscles and raced for the edge. The metal held stronger than I'd thought it would, though the noise of me landing on the neighboring building was quite louder than I'd hoped. Okay…next time, aim for the roof itself.

Once I had my shoes back on, I slipped through the darkness for the roof access door. It took me barely more than a minute to pick the flimsy lock and head into the hall. The stairs started almost immediately, and I gave myself a few seconds to let my eyes adjust. No light, no sound, no strong scent of humans on the air—nothing in my way. No evidence of a security system either. Still, I kept the hood of my sweatshirt jacket pulled up. Better safe than sorry.

Down one flight and through an access door I raced. The top floor seemed empty when I arrived, every office door closed. Every light turned out except for one at each corner. This part would be the most dangerous. If someone remained on the floor, there was no place for me to hide if they happened past. I had to hurry. Use my senses. Hope and pray. Move silently down the long-ass hall until I reached the door I needed, picked the lock, disabled any alarms, and snuck inside.

Yeah, that was all.

With a deep breath and a long, low growl from my inner wolf, I took off. One step after another, silently eating up the space between me and my destination while letting my enhanced senses monitor the area around me. No people, no sounds, nothing that seemed like a threat. So far, so good.

When I reached my destination—the office of Morgan and Fisher, LLC—I paused, checking my surroundings again. Still quiet—still dark. On to the next step. Actually getting inside.

That's when I ran into my first problem. The lock on the door looked different from all the others I'd passed. Tougher and more professional. There was even a small, green pin light shining from the bottom. Some sort of electronic monitoring that hadn't been on the plans, the permits, or the notes.

"Shit," I hissed. Determined, I headed to the unit next door. No pin light, no crazy lock setup. Just a standard handle set—I could manage that. I picked the simple tumbler lock and slipped inside, the door making no noise as I closed it gently behind me. Then I scoped out my options. Ceiling? No, it wasn't a drop one, so there'd be no access. The vents weren't big enough for me to crawl through either. The window on the other side of the room called to me, though, so I hurried across the carpeted space and looked outside. There wasn't really a ledge—the building wasn't that old—but there was enough of a decorative lip on the sill for me to get a toehold.

Balancing on it would be hell, but there weren't a lot of other options, so…

"Outside, I go."

I slipped off my shoes and headed out, clinging to the top of the window for support. My muscles screamed with every step, my balance in question with every inch crossed. But I was crossing them. Not an ideal situation, but workable.

The window to the office next door shared the same lip, which was actually not a sill but a continuing piece of brickwork spanning the length of the building. The designers probably sold it on the architectural interest and depth it offered. I doubted they had any idea a wolf shifter could use it to access any office from the outside. Of course, I still had to not fall to make that true.

Eight terrorizing feet and a whole lot of sweating later, I stood against the window of the office I needed access to. I pressed my face to the glass, hoping for some sign of… something. Sadly, there was nothing obvious. No wires, no panels, no sign of how strong the security could be. There was just a panel next to the door with a keypad on it. Totally generic. Could be a good sign…or not.

I also couldn't see the idol, though Red had mentioned it would likely be stored on a bookshelf. That would be facing the door, not the window. Of course.

Disappointed but not defeated, I inched my way back to the other office, cursing that fucking sill the entire way. Once inside, I took a few seconds to stretch out my screaming calves before heading for the door. Not the most informative recon mission, but it was something. I could make a plan off of what I'd learned. A little calmer than my first trip through them, I slipped down the halls and up the stairs to the roof. This time, I made the jump to the neighboring building from the metal HVAC unit to the rooftop. The stones bit into my hands as

I landed, scraping across my skin as I rolled. Silent, though. Better choice. Besides, the pain didn't stop me from jumping to my feet and running for the fire escape.

Back on firm ground, I grabbed my bag from under the dumpster and headed down the alley for the main street. I'd just made the turn into the space between the two buildings—the same space I'd jumped over earlier—when something made me stop. A scent I'd know anywhere, a tug inside my chest that normally brought me such happiness but tonight infused me with only dread.

Shit.

"Julian?" I inched closer to where I knew he had to be, my heart suddenly wanting to pound straight out of my chest. "What are you doing here?"

He appeared from the shadows. "I was going to ask you the same question." His voice sounded darker than I'd ever heard it, filled with something that made my heart drop into my shoes. Anger.

I took a deep breath, stopping a mere two feet in front of him. "How did you get here?"

"I'm not helpless."

Yep. Definitely anger. And if I knew Julian—which I did—more than a little hurt.

"I know you're not helpless," I said, keeping my voice low and controlled. Not wanting to poke the bear…or human in a bear-like mood. "I would never say you were helpless, Julian. You know that. I just—"

"You just thought you could lie to me and do something stupid and dangerous like break in to the Federal Bank building. What the hell, Angelita? What if you'd been caught?"

The use of my full name hurt. He hadn't called me Angelita when we were alone together since I'd shifted human after my wolf freeze year. At least, not until I'd started lying to him because of this plan of mine. That name, that single word once again used against me for the second time in a week broke my resolve to keep my plan a secret. "I'm trying to keep us together."

"By going to jail?"

"By starting a business."

His brow came down, and he visibly recoiled in what had to be shock. "What?"

Time for the truth. "Remember the shifter who came to the house? Who wanted the Feral Breed to help him with something?"

"The bear shifter?"

"Yeah. He was looking for an idol to secure his pride's matings."

Julian released a deep breath, the sound of frustration loud in the otherwise silent alley. "So you thought you'd break in to a building and get it back for him."

"Not really." Calm, cool, logical. I had to focus on those three things. And making sure my mate knew what I did was for him. For us. "I went to meet the guy the other day."

"When you were supposed to be at the bookstore."

"Yeah. Right. The day I went to the bookstore. I tracked the bear down and offered my services as a bounty hunter to bring back his idol."

"You're not a bounty hunter."

"I'm going to be." I reached for Julian, unable to resist. Needing to feel his hand in mine. Thankfully, he acquiesced. "I'm good at this. I've been sneaking out of Bez's compound for years. I've broken in to local businesses to use their Wi-Fi, hacked in to records offices and private companies just to prove I could, and managed to figure out the basic security systems I've come across. I can do small jobs like this."

"And if you get found out? If the police catch you?"

"I don't exist, remember?"

He was silent for a long time. Too long.

"I did this for us," I whispered, tugging on his fingers. "I started Feral Breed Bounty Hunting so we can stay together. If I make enough money, no one can tell us we can't do what we want. We can live together, you can go to school, everything will be perfect."

Julian sighed, pulling me close. Running his hands up and down my arms as if I was cold. "Leelee, I love you, but this is crazy."

I dropped my head against his chest. "I just want us together."

"I do too, but this is dangerous. And you didn't tell me. How can I keep you safe when you won't tell me what's going on?"

"Maybe I don't need you to keep me safe."

His hands stopped, and his words grew harder. Angry again. "I'm not fucking *helpless*."

I kept myself pressed against him, knowing he needed to feel me. Knowing there was no way to impart my feelings on this without words and physicality. "You could get hurt. You could get arrested, and you do exist in their system. You're human."

"Say it," he said, his body not responding to mine.

"Say what?"

"Say the words. Tell me the real reason you didn't want me to know was because I'm blind and useless to you."

I gasped, unable not to. Julian had never said such things before, had never even seemed as if his lack of sight affected him much. He was fiercely independent and strong—

I couldn't even finish my thought. As soon as the word independent rolled through my head, I knew I'd screwed up. By not involving him, I'd taken away his choice to participate or not. I'd underestimated him.

"You're wrong," I said, scrambling internally to pull words together to fix what I'd broken.

"Don't lie to me." Julian grabbed my arms, his hands tighter than usual. Rougher. He spun me around and pressed me against the wall, boxing me in. Looming over me in a way he never had before. His breathing ragged, his lips turned down in what I could only describe as a sneer. And though the timing was all wrong, though we were literally arguing in a dark alley, the beast inside of me awoke with a need so strong, I whimpered.

Julian cocked his head, suddenly looking more wolflike than I could handle. Fuck, why was that so hot?

"Julian," I whispered, arching into his body. My plea must have ignited something in him. He lunged, slamming his lips onto mine in a way that hurt. In a way that ached. In a way I loved. My hands flew up into his hair, my one leg sliding up his thigh to pull his hips into mine. He didn't kiss me gently or softly—no, he fucking raided my mouth. His tongue demanded mine dance with it, his teeth reprimanded my lips when I didn't respond the way he wanted. Completely aggressive and in control.

With a groan that sounded way too close to a growl, he grabbed my ass and squeezed, yanking me tight against him. The brick wall bit into my back and the noise of the street at the end of the alley filtered through, but I didn't care. Let Julian scrape my skin. Let those people look down and see us. All I cared about—the only thing that mattered—was Julian and his need. And mine.

"I don't need you to protect me," Julian said on a gasp as he pulled away from me. He didn't give me time to respond. He gripped my hips and spun me, pressing his body against my back. My hands hit the rough wall as he reached up and grabbed my breast. Squeezing it. Kneading it in a way that almost crossed the line from pleasure to pain.

So close.

"Juli—"

"Don't shut me out." He slid his hand into the front of my pants, his long fingers finding my clit with practiced ease.

"I won't." I gasped and spread my legs, giving him room. Wanting him to do more than use his hand. It didn't take long for him to completely overpower me. He surrounded me—his scent, his heat, his flesh. His hand on my breast continued its assault, pinching and thumbing my nipple every now and again before going back to gripping me hard. But it was the one in my pants that truly brought out the animal in me. Every stroke a revelation, every push a demand. He was going to make me come right there in that alley.

"Fuck, Leelee. You're so wet already." Julian hissed and rocked his hips against mine. So hard already, so needy. I wanted to spin around and take him in my hand, wanted to drop to my knees and let him fuck my mouth. I wanted that hard cock to be mine in any way he'd give it to me, but his fingers stroking my clit were too good. The feelings he gave me too strong. I could only try to grip the brick wall, gasping and sweating and shaking, as he played my body right over the edge of reason.

"Julian." It was a simple word, a simple plea. One he understood. As if rehearsed, he pinched my nipple and my clit at the same time, pressing his chest to my back and driving me right into the wall. I came with a muffled yelp, rocking over his hand, bucking and growling and completely losing control of everything. Julian stayed right with me, his hands still working me until I had to push him away. Until I couldn't take a single second more.

Until I was utterly, totally sated.

"Where did that come from?" I asked as soon as I'd turned around to face him once more. Julian wiped his fingers on his jeans, still looking irritated. Looking…aroused.

"You don't get to hide things from me," he said, ignoring my question.

Guilt pinged inside of me, and I nodded even though he couldn't see me. "Okay. I'm sorry. It won't happen again."

"Good." He looped an arm over my shoulders and pulled me into his side, directing me down the alley toward the street. "Let's get out of here."

But I didn't want to go home. Every inch of him screamed his need. Every move sharper than normal. I could see the shadow of his hard cock through his jeans, knew he needed relief. And I wanted to give it to him.

I reached over, running my fingers along the length of him behind his fly. "Or we could stay. I could—"

"No." He pushed my hand away, but before I could even register the hurt that move caused, he grabbed my fingers and pulled them to his mouth. One kiss, two…soft touches of his lips against my skin. Soothing the harshness of his actions. "Not here. My friend is waiting to take us home."

"Oh," I said, hearing the sadness in my own voice as if it were someone else's. "I understand."

"No, I don't think you do." He dropped one hand to grab my ass, squeezing hard. Making me jump. "I want to come in your mouth, Leelee. I want you on your knees as I fuck your face, but not in some filthy alley. And not where anyone could see you."

My knees had never felt so wobbly. "I want that—"

"Julian. Over here." A young guy—dark hair, glasses, with a killer set of dimples—hopped out of a small, totally generic sort of car and hurried over. "Hey. I'm Mason."

"Hi," I whispered, still too strung out on Julian's words to focus on anything else.

"Thanks for staying," Julian said as he let me direct him into the car. "We really need to get home."

"Yeah, sure, man. Whatever."

I crawled in the back seat after Julian as Mason raced around to the driver's side. Julian grabbed my thigh and yanked me closer, hanging his arm over my lap in a way that hid the fact that he'd draped his hand down between my legs. He rubbed his pinkie against where I was still so wet for him, so swollen with need. And sensitive. Every swipe made me want to jump, every press almost drew a scream from me. He was such a tease.

But so was I.

As Mason prattled on about something to do with some class they'd apparently both taken, I leaned into Julian's side and placed my hand in his lap. The muscles in his legs clenched as I ran my palm over the length of him, his breath catching as I circled the top before pressing back down.

"You sure you don't want me to stop somewhere?" Mason asked suddenly, his eyes meeting mine in the rearview. "Julian said earlier you hadn't really eaten dinner, Angelita. I can hit a drive-thru."

"No thanks, man. We really just want to go home." Julian didn't swipe that time. He grabbed. Cupping my pussy in a way that caused a small aftershock of pleasure to ripple up my spine. "In fact, take the pay bridge. I've got the money, and it's faster."

Game fucking on.

TEN

Julian

MY CONTROL VACILLATED, ROSE and ebbed depending on the situation. My anger at Angelita for putting herself in danger? My need to claim her and make her mine again? Those restricted my control. Blasting through it until there was nothing but her and me and my need for her. My desire to feel every inch of her flesh.

Fuck the rules and the guidelines and respecting anyone else—she was mine, my mate, and I was going to make sure everyone knew it.

She raced up the stairs ahead of me, her footsteps light and quick as we headed to my apartment. Our apartment. The place where I lived alone almost the entire year. A place where she was staying with me while she visited this last time. I was done with visits. Hopefully, so was she.

"Julian, what—"

I pounced on her before she could finish her sentence, herding her up the last of the stairs to the door. I'd been hard since the alley, since I got her off on my fingers. I could still smell her on them, had all the way home, and that fact drove me crazy. Control? What control? I'd lost mine somewhere between her lying to me and my finding out the truth. The crazy, ridiculous, completely unbelievable, and yet totally Angelita's style, truth.

As soon as the door closed behind us, I pulled away. "I want you naked. Now."

She made that sound again, the one like in the alley. The slight noise that sounded so much like a whimper, and I nearly came right then. Had that sound come from pain or fear, I was sure my body would react differently. But it wasn't either of those—that sound came from desire. Pure and simple. She wanted me. She wanted to come again. And she liked me telling her what to do.

The rustle of clothes broke the silence of the room, the sound of fabric sliding over skin. Of clothing disappearing. Good. I clenched my jaw and stood there, so close I could feel her body heat, far enough away to not touch. Waiting for her to finish. For her to give me a signal. Keeping my drive to slide inside her tight, hot body and pound her on a tight fucking leash.

"Julian," she whispered, her voice shaking. Again, not fear. No. My baby needed. Grew desperate as she waited. I knew that feeling.

"What am I going to do with you, Leelee? You tell me we can't complete the mating even though I ache to claim you and to be claimed by you. Did you know that? My need to sink my teeth into your flesh and bond us together is just as strong as yours. It's painful, and I'm getting tired of waiting. Especially when I know you'll spread those legs for me. You'll take my body inside yours, just not my bite."

She curled against my chest. Sighing when we finally made contact. I wasn't going to lie, I sighed as well.

"I'm sorry," she said, all soft and breathy. "I don't want to lose you. Not to a turning, not to madness, not to Bez pulling me away from here—"

"No fucking way." I yanked her closer, backing the two of

us to the bed. Sitting with her essentially curled in my lap. "I'm done with living apart. We're not doing it again."

"I know." She slid out of my lap, reaching to unfasten my jeans. Her hands eager and direct. "I know, Jul. Let me figure this out. Let me set us up right, and then we can talk about the turning. I want you with me always, I'm just so scared of losing even the smallest piece of your mind."

I lifted my hips to help her pull off my pants. "You won't lose any part of me. We'll get through everything, you just have to—" I stopped breathing as her fingertips brushed across the head of me. Fuck, I couldn't think. Her hand wrapped around my cock, tugging and rubbing and altogether making me feel so good, I thought I could die.

"Lee."

"My turn," she said, and then her hot little mouth stretched over the tip of my cock, her tongue finding its way into my slit. I groaned loud and low, resting my hand on her head as she began to move. Up and down, in and out, all the while sliding her tongue over me when she could. Fuck, she felt so damn good. So perfect. I wanted to thrust, wanted to fuck her mouth. We'd done this before. Hell, last time, I'd gotten a little rough with her and fucked her soft mouth until I came down her throat. She'd loved it, but this was her show. She'd pushed for it, stripped down, and grabbed my cock. I'd let her decide how far to go, how deep. I'd let her own my cock.

And she did.

Suctioning hard, she took me deep into her mouth. Her hands squeezed my legs, and her body writhed against mine. Fuck, it all felt so good, so hot. This was something more than all our times before, something vastly different. The feeling of change danced on the air, of something new between us. One I could practically taste as my body bowed and I came inside my girl's mouth while she fucking moaned around me.

We weren't even close to done yet.

"Fuck." I fell back, panting, still feeling that need and power, still reaching for her. "Claim me, baby. Please."

"Not yet," she whispered, slowly working her way up my body. Dropping kisses on my hips, my stomach, my sternum. I was still half hard, still needing her. Still wanting more. "Just a few more days, Julian. We're so close."

And we were. I could feel it. I knew it. And I was tired of trying to take the high road.

"Come up here." I grabbed her arm, directing her on top of me. Dying a little again when her soaking wet pussy met my quickly recovering cock. "Do you know how much I love you?"

"I know."

"I just want us together."

"That's all I want too."

I thrust again, angling this time. Sliding the tip inside of her. Just the tip. An inch, really. Still, she moaned.

I kissed her nose, rocking a little deeper. "Don't leave me out of your plans again."

"I won't."

"We're a team."

"Yes. Please." She rocked her hips, forcing me deeper.

"Fuck, Leelee, I can't resist you. Why can't I ever resist you?"

"Because we're meant to be together. We're meant to do this. It's our destiny."

I broke. She was right—this was our destiny, and I was tired of running away from it just because I wasn't getting my way. I flipped her over onto her back, thrusting in deep in the same movement. I knew she didn't have a hymen anymore— we would have long ago taken care of that with all we'd done— but I still wanted that first push to be over quick. Wanted any stretching or adjusting to happen fast so I could get her off.

But when I seated myself deep inside of her, she didn't

whine or whimper. She grabbed hold of my shoulders, wrapped her legs around my waist, and hissed a dark and demanding, "Yes."

My mate needed, and I'd deliver.

"Fuck, I forgot—" I groaned, the clench of her pussy around me too good to ignore. "You gotta do that again. But I forgot the condom."

Angelita squeezed me again, arching her back and clawing at my shoulders as she rode my hard thrusts. "I'm good. I have an IUD, and neither of us has ever…"

"Never. Only you." I licked into her mouth, trying hard to concentrate. "So, we're okay, yeah? We can—"

"Come inside me. Just don't stop."

I was very good at following directions.

I plunged ahead, thrusting, panting, groaning. Trying my damnedest to hang on so I could make her come first. One hand between us so I could keep my thumb on her clit, I worked her over. I fucked her hard and fast.

"Leelee," I murmured, unable to find the words to tell her what I needed to. How I loved her, needed her, had craved this moment for so long. I couldn't find the words, but I couldn't hold back either. Not when she reached up and grabbed my face. Not when she clenched hard around me as she fell into her own orgasm. Not with every inch of my cock buried inside her.

And especially not when she bit my lip before whispering, "Want to feel you come, Julian."

So I did. And as I came, as pleasure exploded in my spine and all through my body, I got a flash. One, single quick flash of light. Something I hadn't seen since before the accident.

I got to see…shadows.

"Angelita," I whispered before collapsing on her. Darkness dragged me under, pulling me into sleep before I could do so much as sigh.

"SO, WAIT, you saw something?"

"I think so." I rinsed the soap out of her hair, trying so hard to keep our bodies connected. "It was a flash. But I think I saw light."

She spun in my arms, rubbing her fingers over my cheeks. "How did this happen?"

"I have no idea."

"Julian, this is huge. We need to tell—"

"Who, exactly?" I turned off the water and handed her a towel before reaching for my own. "Who's going to listen to us when I start off with, *Hey, Angelita and I were fucking up in my room when—*"

She placed a finger over my mouth. "Okay, yeah. Bez would kill you."

"Exactly." I dried myself off, sliding on a pair of basketball shorts once I finished. "It has to be us, our connection. Nothing else makes sense."

Angelita huffed. "I need to finish this job."

I couldn't argue with that, so I only grunted my agreement. Angelita definitely understood it. "We have to stay together."

"We do."

She laid a hand on my cheek and pressed a soft kiss to my lips. "Throw on a shirt, my handsome mate. It's breakfast time."

"Fine, but I'll be pulling off yours later."

Her quiet laugh soothed my nerves…for the moment. "Never said you couldn't."

We headed down to the main house, running into Rebel on the back porch. I could feel his tension, sense his worry, even before I took the first step up.

"Don't let Bez see you two."

No wonder. But Angelita didn't seem to care.

"Can we borrow a car tonight?"

"I guess. Why?"

"We want to go out."

Rebel sat quiet for a moment. Too quiet. "What are you two planning?"

Shit. My turn. "A date."

"I don't buy that."

"You don't really have to," I said with a shrug. Time to lay it all out there…or as much as I was willing to show Rebel. He may have been more understanding than my sister, but he was still her mate. If I told him too much, he'd share it with her. "We want to go on a date. That's the story we're sticking with. Can we borrow the car?"

Rebel hummed, the creak of a chair rocking accompanying the sound. "Don't get me in trouble with your sister. If Bez and Sariel say it's okay for Angelita to drive you two around, then you can take one of the cars."

Angelita grabbed my hand. "They'll say it's okay."

"Good," Rebel said. "You'd better run inside and grab some bananas and granola bars. Now might not be the best time to see anyone else."

"Why not?" I asked.

"Boy, I know your senses aren't as strong as mine, so let me fill you in. The two of you look and smell like you've put in an all-night fuck fest. I'd rather not have to fight Bez to keep him from castrating you this morning. It's too pretty outside, and my mate took too good of care of me earlier for my wolf to function at that level."

Angelita snorted. "Too much information."

"TMI? You think I want to see you two looking like this, knowing what I now know you've been up to? Go…grab food.

Then head back to your apartment. I'll tell them all you came down for breakfast already but were going back for a nap."

God bless the day my sister found that man. "Thanks, Rebel."

"You're welcome. And again, don't get me in trouble with your sister tonight. Whatever you're doing, keep it on the down low and don't get caught."

Wiser words had never been spoken.

ELEVEN

Angelita

DATE NIGHT TURNED INTO another practice run for recovering the idol, this time with Julian helping me. Something I hadn't planned but felt right once we started. He was my mate—of course he should be involved in what could very well be our future business. So long as we did this one job right.

We decided to set up a command post of sorts at a coffee shop down the street from the Federal Bank building I'd be sneaking into. It was a bit more public and wide open than I'd like, but that made the plan work even better. People in coffeehouses late at night tended not to notice the other patrons. They were usually too busy working or flirting or…watching anime, as the guy two tables over seemed to be doing. Huh. Hadn't expected that.

"Sound good?" Julian blew air into the mic of the small headset hanging off his ear. It looked like any other Bluetooth device for hands-free phone use, but it had a partner that shared the same frequency. The range sucked, but the sound was clear. Or so the reviews said.

I strolled over to the display case of novelty mugs, feigning interest in the kitschy and meme-like. "Need an *I'm sorry for what I said before I had my coffee* mug?"

"I don't drink coffee." His whispered response sounded perfectly clear.

I walked a little farther away, heading down the hall toward the restrooms. "If we're going to be hanging out in coffeehouses, maybe you should start."

"It could stunt my growth."

"Doubtful."

"It might make me jittery."

"That could be fun."

"Get back here, Leelee." His chuckle had me grinning, had me rushing back to his side.

"Yes, Julian?"

He leaned forward, his lips obviously seeking mine. Soft and sweet, the kiss he placed on me was nothing if not appropriate. Pity that.

"Let's get this test run done," Julian whispered when he finally broke away. "Then we can make you chant '*Yes, Julian*' a few more times."

Oh. So not appropriate. Much better. I ran my fingers up his thigh, stopping only when he squirmed in his seat. "Just a few?"

"I thought that was you, Angel." The sudden appearance of Red the bear shifter made me do a double take. It also made me grip Julian's thigh a little tighter.

"What are you doing here?"

Julian dropped his hand onto mine, squeezing once. Letting me know he was there.

"Checking up on my investment." Red darted a glance to Julian and offered his hand. "We haven't met. My name is Harley."

Julian held out a hand, not missing the social customs just because he couldn't see the other man's offer. "Julian. I'm Angel's partner."

If he was surprised I hadn't given Red my real name, he

didn't let on. Thank the fates my mate was quick on his feet, or else he could have given me away. Not that it would be that hard to find out who I was. The young female wolf hanging with the Feral Breed Motorcycle Club president? Easy as pie.

Red—well, Harley…I'd have to remember that—raised an eyebrow at me when Julian didn't meet his gaze. I raised one right back. Yes, he's blind. If Harley wanted to start something about that, I'd happily finish it.

"Nice to meet you, Julian." Harley turned his attention to me once again as he took a seat across the table from us. "So what's the plan, little wolf?"

Julian squeezed my leg just as my growl rumbled in my chest, though that wasn't enough to hold back my temper. "I'm not little, and the plan is that I go in, cut the alarm, and steal the idol."

Harley blinked. Twice. "That's it?"

"That's it."

"What about cameras?"

"They're only on the bottom floors for the bank itself. The top ones are private offices, and no one rents more than two units, which means smaller companies. I'm not concerned."

"What about guards?"

"I'll handle them if I have to, though I haven't seen any after the bank closes."

Harley sat back, sighing and shaking his head. "I'm not sure if you're brilliant or more balls than brains."

I gave him my prettiest smile. "I prefer the first option."

His frown twisted. "Yeah, well, we'll have to see about—"

"Why haven't you stolen this thing yourself?" Julian asked, his face firm as he stared blankly in Harley's direction. "I mean… if your family needs it so badly, I'd think you'd be sneaking in yourself, or maybe busting down doors and knocking heads around."

Our bear friend leaned in, dropping his voice until I could barely hear him. "Bears aren't exactly known for our stealth, and we're pretty easy to pick out of a crowd simply because of our size. Besides," he continued as he leaned back in his chair, "if they see me, they'll know my clan stole it, which means they could come back and try to take it from us again. I don't want to risk that. It could end badly for everyone."

"So you hire Angel here to do it instead, even though it could end badly for her?"

Harley smirked, and his voice carried a bit of teasing to it. "She volunteered, son, or didn't you know?"

Julian's smile turned wicked, almost as if egging Harley on. "Oh, trust me. I know everything about this deal from her perspective. I'd still like to know why someone stole your clan's idol, though."

"It's not my clan's idol, specifically." Harley sat back again, flicking invisible lint off his jacket. Looking almost…nervous? "Any clan can use any idol. Most have one that's been with the leading family for centuries, though."

Huh. You learn something new every day. "So this one isn't yours?"

"No, but it'll work just fine for us."

"Where's yours?"

"Destroyed. Interclan war. My sister and I are the only ones who survived."

And just like that, every dark memory of the night my pack was slaughtered came rushing back. Julian reached over, grabbing my hand and holding on tight, seeming to know how the bear's words would affect me. How they'd open up old wounds. Old fears. Old fury that never got resolved.

"I'm sorry," I said, practically shaking with my need to fight, to protect. "I know how that feels."

Harley cocked his head, watching me. Assessing.

"Somehow, I think you're telling me the truth, little wolf. For that part, at least."

Julian wrapped his arm around my shoulders. "She is."

Harley nodded once, his gaze on me changing, growing more trusting. "We have something in common, then, though I'm sorry to say that." He stood from the table, his huge body taking up way too much space in the small seating area. "Be careful, little wolf. I'll be around, but I can't be too near the building for fear of being recognized."

"I've got this."

He smirked again, this time without all the doubt behind it. "I almost believe you."

As soon as Harley walked out the door, I sagged, the stress of the past few minutes heavy on my shoulders. Julian, though, simply looked worried.

Really worried. "What's wrong?"

Julian frowned. "I don't trust him. There's something he's not telling us."

"You're just scared I'll get caught or hurt or something."

He grabbed my hand, cradling it. Raising it to his mouth so he could kiss the back of it. "That's to be expected. I like my mate whole and safe. I really like her willing and wet."

"Julian." My whisper sounded deep and dark even to my own ears, filled with need and excitement. Adrenaline raced through my veins already, heightening my awareness, my senses, my…desires.

Julian must have heard all that. "Test run first, then you can Julian me in that voice all night long."

I leaned in to kiss him, licking into his mouth until he grabbed my hips, before pulling away.

"Tease," he said, out of breath.

"Just a little bit." I sat beside him and pulled up the pictures of the idol from Harley's email again. "Okay, test run time. Here's my plan."

TWELVE

Julian

THE NEXT MORNING, AFTER spending the entire evening on edge trying to pinpoint why Harley bothered me so, I hunkered down for a few hours in my room over the garage. I cleaned, I fixed a loose handle or two on my dresser, and I paced. All because something didn't feel right. Something I had no idea how to fix. And I did it all alone because Angelita had headed to the house that morning. Alone until a knock sounded on my door. The three hard, quick raps told me exactly who had come to visit.

"What's up, Rebel?" I asked as soon as I pulled the door open. If the fact that I knew it was him without his saying a word surprised him, he certainly didn't sound like it. Of course, it wasn't the first time I'd known who was coming before they spoke. With his wolf senses, he understood the value of scents and sounds.

"Just wanted to come see how you were doing." His heavy boots clomped across the floor when I stepped back, his steps stopping somewhere around my desk. "How'd the date go last night?"

"You really here to talk dating with me?"

"No. But there are about a dozen women and kids in my house right now. I needed to escape."

Angelita had gone over to the cottage hours ago to spend time with Charlotte and Sariel. They'd invited the witches—Scarlett and Zuri—so the kids could all play together. Calla, Beast's mate, must have joined them and brought their daughter. Thankfully, I'd escaped shortly before the first temper tantrum had been thrown. Rebel wasn't that lucky, apparently.

"I don't have any beer, but the TV works, and there's probably a game on."

"Thank the fates." He must have sat down, as the creak of my desk chair gave away movement. "There's a documentary on duels in the eighteenth century that I wanted to watch."

Of course he did. A man who earned his road name during the Whiskey Rebellion at the end of the eighteenth century would practically *have* to watch a documentary on duels. He'd also probably pick apart everything that was inaccurate about it.

"See, that reenactment is bullshit. I knew they'd fuck this up."

Yep. Picking it apart.

I sat on my bed, listening to the narrator talk about rules and weapons, about famous duels and ones that changed history, and still, my mind wandered. But as the show moved into talking about seconds—the men brought by each participant to be their spokesperson and make sure the duel was fought fairly—my thoughts narrowed. In the modern era, I would be seen as Angelita's second, yet we were dealing with supernatural creatures. Ones who would have no trouble taking me down without my even knowing they were there. As much as I wanted to protect her, to be all she needed, my humanness hindered me, which meant I needed a plan. One she probably wouldn't be happy about.

"You're being awfully quiet over there," Rebel said, his voice even yet curious.

"Just thinking about Angelita and me."

He paused, silent for a long moment, before asking, "Anything you want to talk over?"

Yes. And yet… "I don't really know that I can."

"Okay." And that was why I got along so well with Rebel. He never pushed. My sister? She'd ask over and over again, growing frustrated when I refused to tell her. Rebel had more patience. More trust. He knew I'd come to him if I needed him. And truly, as much as I hated to admit it, I needed him.

So I talked. "Angelita and I are…doing stuff."

Rebel sorted a laugh. "Yeah, kid. I know. I saw you both post-stuff the other day."

"Not like that."

"So you're not fucking?"

On the bed, on the floor, in the shower, over the desk… "Well, we are. But that's not the problem."

"For a kid your age, sex is always a problem."

"Fine. But it's not *the* problem. Not the one I can't stop thinking about. That one's a little more…dangerous."

The TV clicked off and the chair squeaked, the sound growing closer. "How dangerous?"

"Not too bad. I don't think, at least." I took a deep breath, hoping I wasn't betraying Angelita. "We have this project."

"You're not going to tell me what kind, are you?"

"No." Some secrets had to be kept. "It's supposed to be easy enough. Angelita thinks so."

"But you're not sure."

I gave that statement a good thought, let it settle over me. Let my instincts come up with an answer. One I knew Angelita wouldn't like.

"No."

Fabric shifted as if Rebel was moving. Maybe shrugging, maybe sitting back. "Always trust your gut."

I nodded, having heard him tell me that numerous times over the past few years. And I did—trust my gut, that is. Which was why I had to ask, "What if we needed backup for this project?"

"You going into a fight?"

"No, but…you know how back in your time, if someone dueled, they always had a second."

"Yeah."

"What if Angelita and I needed a second? And it couldn't be Bez. Or you."

"Not me, huh?" Rebel hummed once, the chair squeaking again as he moved. Was he…fidgeting? "Depends on what you need them for. If you want strength and attitude, call Scab. He's an asshole, but he's a loyal asshole who isn't afraid of a fight. He'd have your back and keep your secret. If you want a strategist, call Gates or Shadow. Both of them are smart enough to get you out of whatever the fuck you're getting yourself into."

"Okay. Scab, Gates, or Shadow."

"I'm not done." He inched closer, the wheels of the chair making a crushing sound on the rug. "If it was me, and there was a possibility I needed strength, attitude, and a cunning wit to get me out of shit I couldn't get out of myself? If I couldn't call my whole team and had to rely on one person? I know exactly who that'd be."

He definitely had my attention. "Who?"

"Scarlett."

"I—" No matter how much that answer shocked me—she wasn't a member of the Feral Breed, only mated to one—it also made a lot of sense. Scarlett was a witch, and a damn good one from what I understood. She'd helped Angelita shift from wolf to human after she'd been trapped for so long. She also had an attitude that made her seem ten feet tall and bulletproof at times. Plus, her elemental power was fire, and what animal—

supernatural or not—wasn't afraid of being burned alive? "Makes sense."

Another silence, but this time when Rebel spoke it, he sounded different. Worried, almost. As if the advice that had settled my mind had upset his. "You know you can always come to me if you need help, right?"

"I do, but I also know you could never lie to my sister."

"True."

"I don't want to put you in a position where you'd have to. Or where she'd be pissed that you knew if something happened."

Rebel sighed. "Fuck, kid. If it's that dangerous—"

"It's not. I only wanted to know my options. Just in case."

"If you say so." A ping sounded, and Rebel hissed out another curse. "Shit. I have to go to the denhouse. You remember who I told you to call, and try not to get into any trouble, okay?"

I grinned. "I can't promise that."

"Smartass." He gripped my shoulder, his hand warm and heavy. Comforting, in a way. "You know I'd go with you, right? If you need a second, I'd be proud to back you up."

"I know, and I would totally ask you if I weren't worried it would piss my sister off to no end. I don't want to mess up your relationship."

"Fair enough." He opened the door. "If you need any of my guys, use my name as who sent you to talk to them. They'll help you no matter what, but letting them know I'm cool with whatever you have going on could grease the wheels a little. And make sure you call one of them. If your gut is telling you there could be trouble, believe it and go in prepared."

"I will. Thanks, Rebel."

"Anytime, brother."

When the door closed behind him, I sat up and grabbed my phone. The only problem was, I still had no idea who to call. Everything depended on what we'd come up against the night of the mission, what sort of trouble we might run into. Without knowing that, I couldn't identify our needs. Couldn't prepare to make sure Angelita came home safely.

Which meant I had some major considerations to think over.

THIRTEEN

Angelita

SWEATING. I was sweating hard, which didn't exactly make me look prepared and professional. True, I could dress the part of a thief—skintight black pants, shirt, small tool bag across my body. I'd even pulled my hair back into a bun to hold it in place. Yet my nerves wouldn't settle. Neither would my wolf.

Julian crept up behind me, his hands coming to my shoulders as I watched in the full-length mirror. His face stoic.

"Here" He handed me a small earpiece. One that could come in handy since I wouldn't have my phone. "I'll be listening from the alley."

"The coffee shop."

He sighed, grabbing my hips and pulling me back against his chest. "I need to be closer than that to get reception, and you need backup."

"I don't want you too close, though. I'd never forgive myself if anything happened to you."

He spun me and wrapped his arms around my waist, holding me tight. Holding me up. "Fine. But you'd better be a fucking chatterbox while you can to keep me from moving closer."

By the fates, how I loved this man. "Deal."

"Here. Let me fix this for you." He pulled back and straightened the strap of my tool bag, the one running between my breasts. The one that didn't require him brushing the backs of his fingers over my cleavage to move. The tease.

I raised an eyebrow as he brushed a thumb across my nipple. "Thanks."

His smile was quick—both to show and to disappear. "You nervous?"

No point in lying. "Yeah."

"You can back out."

"No, I can't. This is my chance."

He cocked his head, brows furrowing. "Your chance at what?"

"Freedom. If I can do this, make money helping people and sneaking around to recover things they're willing to pay for, I can be independent. I can move up here, and you can go to school. No one would be disappointed in us or be able to stand in our way."

"Is that what this is about? Leelee, no one's ever going to be disappointed in us. Charlotte wants me to go to school because she sees it opening doors for me later, and I want to get my degree. That doesn't mean I need some life-on-campus bullshit. I'm not the frat guy. I never have been."

I knew that. Of course, I knew that. But doubt was a bitch who never let go. "What if you look back on this time and wish you *had* been the frat guy?"

"I won't."

"How do you know?"

Julian shrugged. So sure. So confident. "Because I know. Now kiss me and tell me if we're backing out."

I rose onto the balls of my feet and pressed my lips to his, licking inside once he opened for me. And just for a second—

for a tiny moment—I thought about stripping everything off and taking him back to bed for the evening. But I had plans for us. Big ones. So I broke the kiss instead. "Not backing out."

"Then let's get this over with." He laced his fingers with mine and pulled me toward the door.

Ready for the final run for the idol.

I HATED CROWDS. "Will you be okay here?"

Julian sat with his latte, seemingly oblivious to the bevy of people sitting around the coffee shop. They were all just so... loud. "No. I should just go with you."

"Not happening."

He grabbed my hip, pulling me closer. "Lee—"

But I had to back away. Had to get my mind in the game. "We've gone over this. If I'm worried about you, I won't be able to do this. I'll make a mistake. Just stay here, be safe, and listen to me babble at you, okay?"

He huffed, his hand curling into a fist. "Fine. But don't be too mad at me."

"For what?"

"Anything."

I'd have questioned him more, but a glance at the clock told me it was time to make my move. I didn't have long to pull this off. "Okay, we can talk about what might make me mad later. I have to go."

Julian yanked me down, almost pulling me into his lap before planting a big, deep kiss on me. One that left me breathless and shaking with my need for him.

When he pulled away, his face looked flushed and his chest heaved. "Be fucking safe, angel."

"Promise."

Though I had no idea how to keep my word on that one.

Walking out the door, I kept up a whispered stream of thought solely for Julian's sake. Litter on the sidewalk, a burned-out street light, and the color of every car that passed—those were the things I talked about. He wanted me chatty? He got me chatty. At least for a few minutes. He didn't comment back, though I could hear him breathing in the background. Noticed a chuckle or two as well. At least I could entertain him.

It took almost no time to reach the alley between buildings. Once there, I whispered a "going silent" message to Julian. His response came through staticky and too quiet, too much space between us, but I got the gist of it.

"Love you. Be safe."

"I will." I took one last deep breath then pulled the earpiece from my ear. No sense blocking one of my more valuable senses when I'd be needing it inside to make sure no one snuck up on me. Tucking the metal and plastic piece in my bag, I thought through my plan one last time before heading for the metal ladder. I was on the second-floor fire escape when a shadow moved below me.

"I always did think you were a sassy one."

I growled and spun, ready to fight. Ready to defend myself. But the woman who walked out of the dark shadows below wasn't a threat.

"Scarlett?"

"In the flesh." She curtsied, looking far more dangerous than normal in her jeans and boots with her hair pulled back tightly. "So, what's the plan?"

"Excuse me? What are you—" I closed my eyes, hissing a quiet curse. "Julian called you."

"Don't be mad at him. He wants to keep you safe and

alive. Be able to fully mate with his woman so the two of you can have babies and stuff."

"He told me not to be mad at him."

"See? That's two of us saying the same thing. We win." She looked up at the building I'd eventually need to enter, frowning. "You worried about cameras or alarms?"

"No cameras. I'm sure there are alarms because there's an electronic keypad, but I'm relatively confident I can disengage it."

Scarlett nodded. "You know, I can help you out with that."

"You can?"

"Sure. For a price."

A deal with a witch rarely went in your favor, or so Bez had always told me. Still, this was Scarlett—the witch who'd saved my humanity. I trusted her. "What's your price?"

"Don't ever do something like this again with just Julian as backup. As strong and independent as he is, he's still human. If something were to happen to you, it would kill him that he might not be able to help you." Her face serious, her voice hard, she made her final point. "It would *kill* him."

As much as I hated to admit it, I knew those words couldn't be more right. "Fine."

"Good. Now, go be Spiderwoman or whatever superhero is cool these days. Shadow will be pissed if he figures out where I am. The man is like a human tracking device when it comes to me." She cocked her head, her brow furrowing. "Well, not really human. Not really wolf, either. Tiger-wolf-human tracker."

I...had nothing to say to that. "You're babbling."

"I am. How did we let that happen? Time to work, little angel."

"What are you going to do?"

Scarlett winked and grabbed the post where the electrical came into the building. She closed her eyes, whispering something I couldn't hear as a strong wind blew through the alley. The air suddenly smelled like a lightning strike, and my wolf whimpered.

Magic.

Magic that got shit done. With an audible pop, sparks flew, and every security light in the building went out.

"Blessed be, young one." Scarlett took a step back, grinning when she turned my way. "For your sake, I'm going to hope the guy doesn't have a backup generator in his office. Now go, so I can update Julian."

Thoughts of my mate swirling in my head, I went. Climbing, jumping, racing up, over, and into the Federal Bank building. I had a much better chance of sneaking in and out without notice with the power out, one I couldn't squander. So I hurried, even as I stalked slowly down the stairs and into the hall. As I approached the door to the office where the idol sat.

Dropping to my knees, I slipped a tool kit out of my bag. It held a myriad of metal sticks and pokers, some with curled ends, some grooved. I selected the one I was most comfortable with and set out to pick the lock on the door. Sweat dripped down my forehead as I both tried to concentrate on the lock and keep an eye on my surroundings. There was nowhere for me to hide if someone came down the hall and no way for me to disappear.

Locks tended to have a mind of their own, a personality. Some were stubborn and refused to give until you spent half an hour convincing them. Some needed to be seduced with soft touches and easy strokes. Others required a little added force to pop. The lock I needed to disengage decided to cooperate with me that night, clicking into an open status within just a few minutes of me prodding it. Seemed like a good omen to me.

I pulled my hoodie up around my head, covering my face, before slowly opening the door and creeping inside. No alarms sounded, but that didn't mean anything. There could be a signal being sent to the office's owner right then. He could be minutes away. It was my time to move.

With quiet steps, I walked to the bookshelves…and froze. The idol was missing.

I scanned each shelf again, my heart racing as I came up empty. Oh no, this couldn't be happening. All the work, all the effort. The risk. And it was gone? Where could it have been taken and why? What would I tell Harley? I'd failed through no fault of my own, but it still stung.

Eyes burning, stomach sick, I took one more look around the room…

And nearly cried in relief when I spotted the carved wooden figure sitting on the desk across the room.

Fucking A, way to give a girl a heart attack. I kept my head down and my hood up as I hurried toward the desk and grabbed the idol. Once it was in my hand, I slipped it under the strap of my tool bag and headed for the door. I was done with this job. Almost.

Or so I thought. The scent of bear hit me just before the whispered words did.

"I was hoping you wouldn't get that."

I closed the door to the office behind me, looking over at the familiar strawberry-blonde bear shifter standing just a little down the hall. In my way. "You're Harley's mate."

Her painted lips turned up in a sarcastic smile. "Whatever gave you that impression?"

"I saw you…at the hotel with him."

"Yes, but that doesn't make us mates. I'm his sister, Shiloh."

Huh. Okay, then. "Why don't you want the idol?"

Her eyes dropped to the figurine against my chest, looking sad and almost lost. "Because it's not ours."

"So? I thought you could use any idol to complete your matings."

"Have you ever driven someone else's car or used their computer? The technology works the same in theory, but the feel isn't quite right." She shook her head slowly, her eyes locked on the statue. "That idol will help our clan mate and have babies, but the matches won't be quite right. Our true mates won't be the ones picked because the magic isn't meant for us."

That struck me hard. I couldn't imagine my life without Julian in it, couldn't even begin to think about being tied to someone else. He was my heart…half of my soul. My love.

"That sounds—"

"Depressing as fuck?" She raised an eyebrow. "Yeah, it sort of is. Especially since I know who my mate is, but we won't be together if *that* idol falls into the hands of my brother. We need our clan's idol."

"But Harley said your idol was destroyed."

Her inner bear seemed to push forward—face hardening, wicked curl appearing on her lip, and menace pouring from her body. She may have been pretty, but she was also scary as fuck when she was pissed. And apparently, something about her brother and their idol pissed her right off.

"He lied."

If she expected me to be surprised, she'd be disappointed. "So if it's not destroyed, where is it?"

She lifted a chin toward the door behind me. "That lawyer guy? The one whose office you busted into? It's at his house."

My wolf growled low, both of us knowing where this was going. What was coming. Still, I had to ask…

"Which is where?"

"On the same island where your mate lives, little wolf."

FOURTEEN

Julian

THE WAIT FOR ANGELITA turned out to be much longer and harder than I'd expected. I'd gone in knowing I'd be nervous, understanding that she had planned to complete her mission without my help. Fine. I was man enough to give my woman room to do her thing…just not so much that I couldn't jump in if she needed me to. Which was why I'd called in Scarlett to be her second.

Angelita must not have needed me to, though. She'd been silent for a long time, as had the witch backing her up. Too silent.

I dug deep, trying to feel my bond to Angelita. To locate that same warmth from the link between us I always felt when she was near, but there was no warmth. Only static and…cold.

Scarlett's unique ashes smell greeted me, but it was her voice that set me on edge. "We have a problem."

"Is she okay?"

"I'm not sure."

"What do you mean, you're not sure?"

A pause. A long one. But then she quietly said, "She's gone."

A boulder the size of my entire island landed in my gut—at

least, that's what it felt like as my stomach tightened and the floor dropped out from under my world. "Gone where?"

"Quiet down. People are looking." She grabbed my arm and tugged me closer, lowering her voice even more. "She took forever, so I went to check on her like you told me to do. The office was empty, and there was no sign of her anywhere in the building."

There was no thinking to be done, no decision to be made. There was only one goal. "We have to go find her. We're going to need help."

"I know. I already called Shadow. He's pissed at me, but he'll be here in a minute. Come on, let's go see what we can figure out."

I gripped her elbow as she led me through the coffee shop and out the door. The night air had grown colder, the street quieter, all while I'd sat and done nothing. Whether it would be the anger or the guilt that ate me alive, I had yet to see. But one would. And soon.

We rushed down to the alley where Angelita would have started and ended her mission, but the bond inside of me never grew warmer. The static stayed, the distance between us too much. And while most of my mind focused on worry about Angelita, a tiny part raged. The base side of me, the instinct. The part that said if Angelita had run into foul play, whoever had put their hands on my girl would regret it. I'd rip them apart with my bare, human hands. I would not lose my mate over some bear clan's fucking mating idol.

I didn't hear Shadow arrive—I rarely heard the man move—but I felt Scarlett tense up next to me and knew that backup had arrived in the form of her half-tiger, half-wolf shifting mate.

"It reeks of bear by the front door," Shadow said, his voice hard.

Scarlett stepped around me, moving closer to Shadow. "Maybe the guy who set this up pulled a switch?"

Shadow grabbed my arm, giving me a squeeze before inching past. "That doesn't fit the scent."

That answer didn't sit well with me. "Why not? You said you scented bear."

"But it's a female bear."

"Are you sure?" I followed Scarlett's guidance as the three of us moved deeper between the buildings. All the way back to the alley that ran along the rear.

Shadow stopped, audibly scenting the air. "Yeah. Female bear, and Angelita got into a car with her. The scent disappears at an empty spot."

"What do we do?" Scarlett asked.

There was only one thing *to* do. "We go see the bear that hired her and find out who took Angelita."

THE GRAND HOTEL WHERE Harley had rented a block of rooms was one of those restored buildings from an earlier era. People raved about how gorgeous all of the shiny wood trim and grand staircase was. I gave no fucks for the history of it—I wanted to know the present. Particularly, the location of one bear shifter. Finding that information out would fall on the shoulders of the witch, though.

Once Scarlett had spelled the desk worker and determined the bear's room, I raced up the stairs and felt the walls for room plates.

The growl I released when I finally found one could have stood up against one of Shadow's for sure. "They don't have fucking Braille."

"Let me help you." Scarlett placed my hand on her elbow and strode down the hall, pulling me with her. I was already pissed because my mate was missing. The fact that I couldn't even find a damn hotel room without help from someone else was merely more shit piled onto me. Which might have been a good thing because by the time Scarlett stopped, I was in a full-blown fury.

"This is it," she whispered.

I didn't pause for a second. Reaching out, I placed one hand against the wood to get my bearings before taking two steps back. Then I kicked the fucking door in.

"Where is she?" I yelled as soon as I stepped inside. "Where's Angel?" My voice caught on her shortened name, my need to keep her safe overriding everything I knew.

"Who the fuck…" the bear growled low and deep, the sound of him growing closer making the hair on my neck stand on end. "You're the little wolf's mate."

He must have moved too fast because Shadow snarled from behind us as Scarlett edged around me.

"You'd better stay back, bear," Scarlett said, then the smell of burning paper exploded through the room.

"You work with witches?" Harley asked, his voice high and angry. "That's bad form, old friend. Witches are quite undesirable."

"I'm not your friend, and this witch could burn you alive from the inside if she wanted to. So you'd better start answering my question. Where's Angel?"

The bear huffed a sarcastic laugh. "Did your girl get caught?"

"No, she got taken by a female bear shifter." I stepped closer, my anger driving me. My focus locked on bringing Angelita home. "Any idea who that could be?"

Harley roared, his animal side obviously taking over before he raced past me and out the door. Scarlett grabbed my elbow and followed the huffing, pounding footsteps.

"Did he shift?" I asked quietly, unsure what to expect.

"No. But he looks close to it."

"Can you handle a full-grown bear?"

Shadow scoffed. "Kid, you have no idea."

"And this is why you'll be rewarded later, my love." If Scarlett's voice could have been more sarcastic, I had no idea how. "Fire is a base fear, kid. I've got this if he shifts."

Okay, then.

Harley must have knocked another door down because the sound of the wood splintering broke like a gunshot. "Motherfucker. I'm going to kill her."

He wasn't the only one who could growl. "You'd better not be talking about my mate."

"I'm talking about my sister." He huffed a breath, hurrying past me once more. "Come on. I know where they went."

Scarlett squeezed my arm as if to argue, so I said the only thing I could. The only thing that mattered in that moment. The only word I knew would keep her moving.

"Angelita."

And so she led me to follow after the bear.

FIFTEEN

Angelita

THE PLACE WHERE SHILOH took me wasn't a house. Huge and sprawling, it ate up the shoreline and blocked the view of Canada from the road. I couldn't even see the end of the house from where I stood…it just kept going.

Not a house. A fucking mansion. "This guy's a lawyer?"

She huffed, obviously buying that story as much as I did. "Yeah. An expensive one who deals in getting companies off after being sued by the workers they injured."

"Oh, that sucks."

"Big-time, but that's not what we're here to deal with. Come on. You can see the idol from the other side of the house."

"You're awfully familiar with this place."

"I did what I needed to do to track my idol down."

What she needed to do… That sounded an awful lot like… "You…had a relationship with this guy?"

She paused, her face stiff and expressionless. Her eyes fierce, though. "You have a mate, yes?" At my nod, she cocked her head. "How far would you go to be with him? To secure that mating bond and spend the rest of your life by his side?"

I opened my mouth to speak, but the words wouldn't come,

too bogged down by guilt and regret. I'd been refusing Julian—my one and only mate. I'd been stopping us from completing our bond because I was too afraid to turn him. Too afraid to lose him. Shiloh had no such fear. She'd forced herself to step away from her mate, to spend time with another man. A short-term hell in exchange for a long-term heaven.

When I didn't speak, her lips twisted into a smirk. "You have a lot of growing up to do, little wolf."

I couldn't argue that one.

Conversation over, we snuck around the side of the house until we reached a window looking into what appeared to be a sort of library. An older man sat behind a desk, working on a computer with his back to us. Oblivious. At least fifteen idols—all very similar to the one I had against my chest—sat on the bookshelves almost directly across the room from him… and us.

So many look-alike statues. "He sure does like your idols."

"I think he has some bear shifter in him from generations back. He collects a lot of our stuff."

"Really? That seems weird."

"It happens. Shifters breed with humans, those babies stay in their human world, the shifter genes get diluted until the next generation can't shift at all, and then one day you end up with a human who has an obsession for artifacts of shifter cultures he doesn't actually know exist."

"Yeah. Like I said. Weird." I inched closer, inspecting each idol as well as I could from the distance. "I hope you know which one is yours. Otherwise, I'm going to need a great big bag."

Her eyes never wavered. "Second shelf, right side, third one in. That's ours."

I found the idol in question, memorizing its placement. Its details. Committing it to my mind so I wouldn't pause once inside. "I'll put the fake one in its place—give us a little extra time to get away from here."

She glanced at me, her brow furrowed. "That's a good idea. You're smarter than I thought, wolf."

"Never doubt me, bear. You're doing all this for your mate. I have the same motivation."

"Then we're on the same page." She backed up, tucking herself into the bushes. "He goes for a cup of tea every night. We just have to wait for him to want it."

I eased back, watching. My blood pounding in my ears. Julian had to have figured out I wasn't where I was supposed to be by now. He was probably freaking out with worry. The useless earpiece sat in my bag, but not my phone. I'd left that at the apartment like an idiot. I had no way to actually talk to my mate from so far away. Next time—

I bit my lip to keep from grinning. As stressful as all this was, I knew there'd be a next time. Another target. Another mission. But when we signed on for that one? I'd make sure Julian was by my side the entire time. Or at least, in my ear. We just needed better technology.

I almost yelped when the man stood up from his desk, the motion fast and abrupt enough to shock me right out of my thoughts. Time to get this mission completed.

Shiloh grabbed my hand, practically vibrating in place. "You've got about seven minutes to grab that idol and get out."

"Is there security?"

"Tons, but no cameras and the perimeter stuff is off when he's home. When he leaves, he arms the doors and windows." She pulled me closer, making sure every word carried the weight of its importance. "Seven minutes, tops. I'm not rushing in there to save you if you screw up."

I really needed to work with wolves and not bears. Loyalty must have skipped right over their breed. "Seven minutes, 420 seconds. Got it."

I walked right up to the tall window in front of me. A crank lever sat inside, tucked against the frame. Grabbing a couple of long, skinny metal pieces from my tool kit, I went to work on the edges, counting the entire time. At 147 seconds, the seal popped, and I was able to pull the window open.

I stood inside the office at 164 seconds.

Made it to the bookcase at 229.

Switched the idols at 315.

But at exactly 403, the plan went to shit.

"What do you mean the power's been down for almost an hour? You should have called me sooner." The man rushed into the office just as I slipped behind a chair along the side wall. He had his phone to his ear, probably talking to security at the Federal Bank building on the mainland. Scarlett's little trick with the electricity must not have been temporary.

The man yanked open a drawer on his desk, grabbing something that jingled…keys, probably.

"I'll be there in ten minutes. Guard my fucking office until then. Do you understand?"

He stomped out the door, and I sagged against the chair in relief. Well, at least until Shiloh's words about the security on the house played through my head. Fuck, he was leaving…which meant he was about to arm the house.

I raced full out for the window, diving through it just as I heard a door open somewhere in the house. Thankfully, Shiloh stood ready on the other side of the glass, her hand at the top. She slammed the window closed as soon as I rolled into the bushes outside. Two seconds later, the hum of the alarm going on made my ears twitch.

But I had the correct idol in my hand. "That was close."

Shiloh huffed, ducking into the bushes next to me. "Yeah. Just a bit."

"So seven minutes for tea, huh?"

"So you killed the electrical to the entire building where his office is, huh?"

"Guilty." I rolled to a sitting position, clutching the idol to my chest. "Shit, I need to get back to the original job site."

"You can't. He'll be down there, looking for anyone suspicious. And no offense, wolf. You're suspicious as hell dressed like that."

Okay, yeah. Skintight, all black, and a cross-body tool kit wasn't exactly a fashion statement. "I have to. My mate is waiting for me close by." Waiting…without a way to reach me. I blew out a breath, dreading the fight I was sure would be coming my way. "Julian's going to be freaking out."

"Julian passed freaking out forty-five minutes ago."

My mate stepped into the bushes, followed closely by Scarlett. Shadow stood back, nearer to the tree line and living up to his road name as he almost blended into the darkness. Harley stood at his side, scowling my way. Not blending at all. And looking as if he was about to shift and go for blood. Thankfully, all that ire seemed to be directed at his sister. Sucked to be her, but I had my own issues to contend with.

Namely, one very pissed-off mate.

SIXTEEN

Julian

WE LEFT SCARLETT AND Shadow on the island as we followed the bears to their hotel. Something about finalizing the details, though I was in no mood for such things. I just wanted—no, needed—to get Angelita home. To run my hands over every inch of her and make sure she was safe. To deal with the fact that she'd casually knifed me in the heart by leaving me behind.

So yeah, no time to deal with the bears. And yet, there we stood.

"Thank you so much for all your help. You've honestly given me such a gift with this." Shiloh sounded genuine, completely satisfied with Angelita's work. Good. She damn well should be considering the girl technically did two jobs for her and her brother. "I hope to see you again sometime."

Never, but Angelita was more diplomatic than I was at the moment.

"A mate for a mate, that was the deal," Angelita said. "But next time, try to get the habits of the guy we're stealing from right."

"Or try not to knock out an entire building's electricity."

"I make no promises."

Harley huffed, his voice like gravel. "Yeah, thanks for getting the idol, little wolf."

Nope. Not getting away with that. "Two idols."

"Two idols." At least he agreed with me. The sound of clothes rustling reached my ears, and then the bear sighed. "A deal is a deal, though two events make this a more valuable transaction."

"How valuable?" Angelita asked. There wasn't an answer, just the scratchy sound of fingers on something rough. And then her breath whooshed out of her. "Okay, so *really* valuable."

Money. Harley must have paid her for her work.

He laughed, the roughness of his voice grating. "Don't be so obvious next time, kid. I'd have paid you more if you'd asked for it."

"I could ask for it now."

"Don't push your luck." His voice changed, and his footsteps drew nearer to me. "Goodbye, Julian. It was nice to meet you."

Angelita touched my elbow, and I reached forward, offering my hand. Harley grabbed it in his meaty one, surrounding mine completely, and shook.

"You've got quite a mate there," he said, but he had no idea.

"Yeah, I know."

"Be thankful, son. The fates don't bless all of us so easily." He withdrew his hand. "Take care of her."

And wasn't that like pouring gasoline on a flame? "I would if she'd ever let me."

Angelita grabbed my hand, holding tight as the three of them finished up their small talk and said their goodbyes. Me? I burned beside her. Something dark and scary bubbling up inside me. Something that had taken hold and drowned out the fear the moment I knew Angelita was all right. And I was ready to let it boil over.

We were headed down to the parking lot where the car we'd borrowed again from Rebel sat waiting for us when Angelita asked, "Are you really mad?"

I had no words for how much. "Furious."

"I wasn't trying to keep you from the job."

"Yes, you were." When we reached the car, I opened Angelita's door for her, even though she would be driving, then hurried to the passenger side to get in, keeping my fingers on the warm hood since I'd forgotten how many steps I needed to move across the vehicle. Counting was such a habit at this point, practically an instinct. The fact that I hadn't only exemplified how thrown off I'd been by her actions earlier.

As I slipped inside, Angelita whispered, "Do you need me to—"

And the chain around my temper broke. "I'm not fucking helpless, Angelita. I don't need you protecting me all the time."

She didn't respond at first. Didn't acknowledge my words as she started the car and pulled out of the lot. She didn't speak again until we made it to the bridge.

"I know I was wrong, Julian. I shouldn't have left without you, and I'm sorry."

The boiling eased, but I held fast to my anger. I wasn't ready to give in yet, to accept. Or maybe I was just ready for something else. Another form of hashing things out. If the fact that my cock was so hard it leaked were any indication, then we'd deal with our disagreement in bed.

She needed to drive faster.

"Do you want to know how much money we made?" Angelita asked as she made a turn that had to be onto the lake road.

"No." Three minutes. We'd be home in three minutes, then she was mine. I could lay out how much she hurt me, give her a chance to apologize, then sink deep inside her and prove to that instinctual part of me that she was all right. Whole. And mine. Always fucking mine.

Angelita sighed, her voice practically trembling. "Do you want—"

"Can we not? I can't pretend I'm not so fucking mad at you right now. If you don't give me a minute, I'm going to have you pull over this car and I'll fuck you right on the side of the road because I can't hold myself back. Just get us home."

Angelita went quiet. Completely, utterly silent other than the quickening rasp of her breath. She knew what I needed, how much I wanted her. Hell, I always wanted her. Wanted to feel her skin under mine as I touched and tasted every inch of her. I'd been terrified that something had happened to her when Scarlett had told me she'd left the job site. Terrified and completely helpless all at once. I'd never felt the loss of my sight as a burden until that moment, sitting in the coffee shop, knowing I couldn't track her down without help. And now, the adrenaline those moments had caused to swell was well on the way to crashing, and my need to prove I could handle her, to reclaim her as mine and fuck her through the mattress, was too strong to resist. There was no way we weren't having sex as soon as we got home. I could practically smell her arousal already, could hear how fast her breaths came. She was in the same boat—needy, desperate, and turned on after the jobs she'd done tonight.

When the sound of gravel under the tires met my ears, I shifted in my seat. I only had about a minute left to wait for her. My cock twitched, ready to bust out of my pants all on its own. Aching and wet with need for my mate. Fuck, I'd never been so turned on, which made everything about the delay that much harder to deal with. Seconds felt like hours, every mile endless.

Until they weren't.

Angelita pulled onto pavement and slowed to a stop. Home. I threw open my door and rushed out of the car, but then I froze. I'd been distracted as she'd pulled in and couldn't figure out which way to go. I closed my useless fucking eyes and sighed.

"Lee. Which way?"

She stood at my side in a second, giving me her elbow and leading me toward the garage. Without a word, she put my hand on the railing of the stairs. Relief settled over me, but that didn't last long. I still wanted, still needed her. I still couldn't wait to taste her all over. I didn't need to see her to give her pleasure, didn't need sight to make her come. To suck on her little clit and fill her pussy until she became a writhing, screaming mess. Which was exactly what I was going to do... once we got inside my place.

We climbed the stairs in unison, my hand brushing hers with every step. About halfway up, she whimpered, the sound going straight to my cock. So I smacked her ass.

"Faster."

Angelita practically ran up the last of the steps while I followed right behind her. Yeah, she was just as ready as I was. Just as primed. Thank God for that.

When I got to the door, I didn't reach for my keys. Instead, I pinned Angelita against it, using my hips to hold her in place. Caging her in with my arms.

I couldn't keep the growl from my voice. "You really pissed me off tonight."

"I know." She trembled under me, the scent of her need telling me it wasn't fear making her do so. It was need. For me.

Slowing down for just a moment, I took the time to run a finger down her face, over her chin, and along her bottom lip. Tugging there just to hear her gasp. "I was so scared and fucking angry that you didn't trust me to help you. That you didn't even tell me you were changing locations."

"I know that too."

I slipped my thumb inside her mouth, nearly groaning when she bit down before sucking it inside. Jesus, fuck, she was going to make me come in my pants if she kept that up. "Don't ever fucking leave me out again."

She released my thumb, whispering, "Never."

I'd take her word…for now. So I handed her my keys, grabbed her hips, and flipped her until she faced the door. Her quiet squeak turned into a throaty moan when I leaned into her body, pressing my cock against her ass.

"Good. Now open this door so I can fuck you until you can't walk."

SEVENTEEN

Angelita

A SHIVER ROCKED MY body, my inner wolf howling in my head. Julian wanted to… By the fates, I couldn't even think it. I couldn't move either. Or speak. Who needed words at that point? Julian stood before me, chest heaving, eyes dark and needy as he stared blankly in my direction. And me?

I'd been set on fire by his dirty mouth.

He hadn't touched me, hadn't kissed me. Hadn't done anything but tell me what he wanted to do, and I was soaking wet. Wanting in a way I never had before—so strong, so desperate. But I kept my distance. Held myself still. The tension blanketed us, practically suffocating me, and still, I waited. For what? I had no idea, but Julian waited too. Both of us on edge. Breathing hard and ready.

I cracked though, when the very tip of his pink tongue flashed. A little lick of his bottom lip. Probably not even something he realized he did. But I saw. I felt that tiny flick right over my clit. And I whimpered.

Julian pounced, his arms wrapping around me and his mouth landing on mine. He offered no lead-in, no gentle touches or softness. He'd become the animal I'd always been, his sexual attraction to me an instinct. One he wouldn't deny.

I tugged his shirt up and over his head, my head falling back as he fastened his lips—and teeth—to my neck. Hands everywhere, he stripped me as well. Both of us rushing, fumbling, backing toward the bed as pants fell and shirts landed across the room. And when we stood naked before each other, bodies pressed so close there was no air between us, I took one moment to make sure he knew how I felt.

"I love you, Julian."

A smile curved one side of his mouth, and he cupped my cheek gently. Lovingly. "I know, and I love you too, Lee. But I'm still mad, and I can't be sweet right now."

I nodded, sinking my teeth into his thumb when he dragged it across my lower lip. With a growl that could have made several grown wolf shifters jealous, Julian picked me up and tossed me on the bed, dragging me to the edge by my ankles before settling on his knees.

"Do you have any idea how panicked I was?" He pushed my knees wide, spreading me before him. Massaging my thighs roughly as he leaned in. "You weren't where you were supposed to be—no word, no info on where to find you. And me?" He licked a long line along the side of my pussy, teasing me. Making me arch and moan before pulling away again. "I was forced to rely on Scarlett and Shadow to take me to the client so I could figure out what had happened. My very heart had disappeared, and I couldn't do anything about it."

"Julian—" I bit my lip as he flicked his tongue against my clit. Each pass rougher, more brutal. Pushing me straight toward my orgasm.

"You want to do this sort of work? You know I'll support you." He slipped a finger inside me, and my legs began to shake. In and out, he dragged that digit, adding pressure where I needed it. Where I wanted it. Where I wanted him. "But, next time?"

Another brush of his tongue against my clit, but this time, he didn't stop. Finger deep in my pussy, he latched on to my clit and sucked. I arched off the bed, practically screaming his name as my orgasm raced through me unexpectedly. But Julian didn't stop; he kept pumping his hand, adding another finger to drag me through that pleasure. Keeping his mouth on my clit to force it higher. And when I was done, when I had to push his head away because everything had become oversensitive, he still didn't stop. Kept his fingers buried and his mouth close enough to feel his breath as he picked up right where he'd left off.

"Next time, we go in with full communication. We invest in technology for me to talk to you, to track you, and to always find you. Because if you change the plans again, and go off on some mission without anyone knowing how to save your ass if things go south?" Quicker than I would have expected, he grabbed my hips and flipped me, pulling my ass into the air as he stood behind me. As he buried himself inside me in one thrust. As he owned my pussy. "If you run off again, I'll still chase you. I'll always fucking find you. But my anger won't be as much fun as this time."

Julian thrust harder, practically pushing me up the bed. Spreading my legs wider and thrusting harder. I grunted with every stroke, clawing at the sheets as I sought purchase. Every muscle tingling, every inch of me ready for another orgasm. For more.

His hand landing in an open-palm smack against my ass was just the *more* I'd been craving. I came screaming into a pillow, shaking and jerking as lights exploded behind my eyes. Julian kept pumping, kept hitting me in all the right spots, even dropping a hand under me to tweak my clit. That little hit caused another smaller orgasm to roll through me, and I collapsed on the mattress. A sated, swollen mess.

Julian pulled out, his hand fisting his cock, still wet from me. Two strokes, and he came all over my ass and back. Grunting through his release as he kept one hand on my hip. As he held my body in place and dominated me. I'd probably have bruises from how hard he pushed me down, but I liked that idea. Liked it enough to be sad about how fast they'd fade.

"Fuck." Julian collapsed beside me, pulling me into his arms. I went willingly, curling around him and using his arm as a pillow. "Angry sex is sort of fun."

I chuckled, my fingers tracing a pattern along his chest. "Are you still mad?"

He grabbed my hand, bringing it to his mouth to kiss my palm. "Furious. But only because I was so scared." He leaned closer, bringing his mouth to mine for a soft, slow kiss that I felt all the way down to my toes. "I can't lose you, Leelee. You're my heart. Without you, even breathing would be impossible."

"Julian…"

But he didn't let me finish. Instead, he rolled on top of me and kissed me deeply. Stoking another flame only our bodies coming together could put out. And I was fine with that. We needed the connection, needed to be sure the other was safe. And I needed to finally surrender to what we both wanted, even if I was terrified of it going wrong. So when he broke from the kiss to run his lips along my jaw, I took a deep breath. And I gave him forever with me.

"I want to give you your wolf."

He froze, muscles stiffening. "Angelita—"

"I want to. To make you a wolf shifter, like me. I want to claim you as my mate in every way."

He relaxed slightly, running his nose along mine. "What changed your mind?"

"You. This job tonight. Shiloh. I don't know…but I don't want to keep pushing this off because I'm afraid things will go wrong. I want you as my equal, and that means giving you this gift." I rolled him onto his back, straddling his hips. Running my pussy along his already hard cock just to tease. "If that's still what you want."

Julian grabbed my hips, holding me tight. "You. I want you. Always. I've never wanted or been so sure of anything in my life."

So I took him inside me, and I rocked. Lifted. Made love to him slowly. Watched as he arched his back and bit his lip, as he gripped me harder, trying to take control of my actions. But I kept my pace, doing everything I could to hide the tears I couldn't hold back. The fear. If I lost him, I'd die. I knew it, and I think somewhere deep down, he knew it. But it was time for us to take a chance. Together.

I leaned over him, pressing a kiss to his neck before whispering, "You're my heart, too, you know. And we do this together."

Hands tight, he thrust up into me. "Always."

And then, with a growl everyone on the island probably heard, with my wolf side taking over enough to grow fur across my body, I shoved us right into our future together.

With my teeth in his neck for the first of our mating bites.

EIGHTEEN

Julian

COLORS AND LIGHT. They inundated me the second Angelita's teeth broke my flesh. My body practically exploded through an orgasm that seemed endless, my hips thrusting almost mindlessly as she rode me through the endless waves of sensation. I couldn't breathe, couldn't speak… The only thing I could do was hang on to her and feel the pleasure ricocheting between us.

But then something other than pleasure hit me. Something that felt like…her.

"Leelee," I gasped, my head thrown back and my body arching. Fuck, Angelita seemed to be just as far gone as me. Snapping her hips back and forth, her moans loud and long. Her pussy squeezing the life out of my cock. Too long, it lasted. Exhausting me.

Fuck, she'd claimed me, and now I needed to do the same.

Weak but recovering quickly, I rolled her over, diving down the mattress to settle between her thighs. I needed a few minutes, just a little time to give my cock, and I knew exactly how I wanted to spend them. Angelita chuckled when I dug my fingers into her thighs, at least until I licked over her clit—

then she gasped and grabbed my head to guide me. I fucking loved it when she did that. I attacked her pussy, licking over the flesh, sucking on her clit, pushing her toward her orgasm. Toward when I would claim her as mine.

Rebel had told me all about claiming bites, had instructed me on how to handle it once Angelita was ready and what I would need to do. He'd been like a father in that aspect, but some of the other Breed members had been more like big brothers. They'd given me all the dirty details. How the orgasms during the bite were the most intense—a fact I'd already verified. They'd also explained how a man should place his bite mark in a place so other men knew his female had been claimed. I'd secretly picked my spot the very first time I'd ever felt Angelita's soft, bare thighs. Long before I'd ever actually gotten her naked.

"Here." I circled a spot high up on her thigh. The little divot that I knew was from her time in captivity. A scar that reminded her of the worst part of her life—one that I wanted to replace with something good. A new memory. "I want my bite to be here."

Angelita grabbed my hair, pulling me closer. "Wherever. Just do it."

I chuckled, kissing my spot before zeroing back in on her clit. "I don't think you're ready yet."

She huffed and arched, tugging on my hair. Directing me. "Please."

"Since you asked so nicely." I wrapped my lips around her clit and sucked, thrusting my fingers deep inside her at the same time. Angelita released a hoarse cry before stiffening up, which was my cue. I dove lower, grabbing her knee and pushing it up and out. Opening her for me. And as she came, as she screamed my name and her muscles locked down, I bit her.

Her entire body jerked, her cry deepening, growing louder. Sustaining as she shook beneath me. Her pleasure washed over me, reverberating through my body, causing me to come again without a single touch to my cock. Both of us sparking off the other. Joined in that moment. And when she finally came down, when her muscles relaxed, she yanked me by the hair to slide up the length of her body.

"We're mates," she whispered before dropping a soft kiss on my lips.

"We've been mates. It's just official now."

"I like official things."

My silly girl. "Me too."

She cuddled into my arms, tucking her head beneath my chin. We still needed to deal with changing me, but I knew that would be hard for her. Angelita feared losing me, and I could understand that. Hell, after the night we'd had, I'd lived such fear. So I gave her the time she needed, stroking her naked back and breathing her in to stay calm.

But eventually, my relaxed mate grew tense no matter what I did. It was time.

"Are you sure about this?" she asked, her voice soft and slightly husky.

"Yes."

"There's no turning back. Once I bite you to turn you—"

"I know. I want it. I want to be able to stand beside you as an equal."

Her breath shook on her inhale. "They took my family, Julian. If they ever come back, if another group decides to repeat that attempted takeover, a human might be able to escape."

I rolled her under me, cupping her face. "If they ever come back, I want to fight by your side, not run. If you can't escape, then neither will I. Live or die…we do it together."

Wetness met my palm, her tears falling as she cried silently. Something that nearly tore my heart out.

"We can wait for you to be ready," I said, even though the words killed me to speak.

But Angelita shook her head. "No, we can't. I may never truly be ready, so tonight is as good a night as ever. So long as you're prepared."

"I am."

She sighed before pushing me off her.

"What are you doing?"

"Calling for backup. We'll do the turning bite alone, but I want others close just in case." Something silky and smooth landed on my lap. "Put something on in case they have to come in."

Once I tugged my basketball shorts into place, I lay back, keeping an arm around her hip as she called Rebel and Bez, Charlotte and Sariel, Scarlett and Shadow. Our friends and family. Our support system. Damn, were we lucky to have them in our lives. No matter how tough they'd been on us, how restrictive at times, I knew they'd show up.

"They'll all be at Rebel's if we need them," Angelita said as she completed her last call. "You're sure?"

"Yes."

"This can't be undone. It's forever."

I traced the indentation from my teeth on her thigh. "So is this."

Angelita grabbed my hand. "Okay. Then sit up."

She slipped behind me, cradling me in her thighs. Her breasts pressed to my back beneath what felt like a cotton shirt, and her lips found the back of my neck. One kiss, two. I took a deep breath and clutched her hand against my chest.

"I love you, Leelee. We're doing this together, just like everything else. You and me. Forever."

Her forehead landed against my spine, and her breath hitched before she whispered, "Forever."

Angelita

HE WANTED FOREVER WITH me. He always had, and if the gods and fates allowed it, he always would.

Rebel had been very clear on what to do. Where to bite to give him the best likelihood of coming through the turning without any issues. I'd known the rules for years, had been reminded of them countless times because Julian was human and therefore a bit more fragile than me. I'd always thought I'd be prepared for this.

I was so not prepared.

But I felt Julian's breaths, felt the warmth of his body against mine. He trusted me, and I couldn't let him down. So I took a deep breath, zeroed in on the spot where I'd bite, and let the memory of Rebel's words guide me.

"Julian?"

"Yeah?"

I allowed my wolf to push forward, fur sprouting over my skin as I shifted to some sort of mixed-up creature. Half human, half not. Thank the fates Julian would never see me like this, for it had to be one hell of a scary sight. My muzzle lengthened, and my teeth grew longer, sharper. More predatory. Claws ripped through my fingertips, making me wince at the prolonged sting, but this was required. I had one shot to do this right, and I wouldn't fail him.

Still, as I pressed my wet nose against the nape of his neck, I growled a rough, "I'm sorry."

He froze for just a second before I surrendered to the animal inside of me, biting him hard right at the top of his spine. He jerked and yelped before sprawling backward against me. Unconscious.

"It's done." I spoke loudly, knowing the people I needed most at that moment—other than Julian himself—were right outside the door. The whole being at Rebel's house thing had been a bit of an exaggeration. One last lie to protect him.

Rebel came through the door first, his worried eyes running over Julian before meeting mine. "Everything okay?"

How to answer such a question? I supported Julian as his body fell onto the mattress, then I got to my feet beside it. "I think so. I don't… I've never…"

And then I broke. I sobbed, tears falling and chest heaving. My mate, my love, my Julian looked dead as he lay still and silent. Strong arms wrapped around me, but not Rebel's. Bez's, and he pulled me into a hug that nearly crushed me.

"He'll pull through this. We'll make damned sure of it."

Rebel rested a hand on my arm. "Absolutely. We even have a witch with us in case something goes sideways."

"I guess I'm the plus one at this party." Scarlett ran her fingers over my cheek before holding her hands out toward Julian and closing her eyes. She stood silent for a long moment, the only sign that she was working her magic the smell of ozone on the air. "It's already happening. His human side is dying, but the animal side is strong and taking up the loss. It shouldn't be too long, though I don't know much about wolf turnings."

"You turned this wolf around just fine." Shadow came up behind her, wrapping his arms around her waist before kissing her neck. "A day, maybe two. That's the norm."

"I'd put my money on him coming through tomorrow, then." She gave me a soft smile. "Anything we can get you? Food? Something to drink? Margaritas would definitely help pass the time."

I laughed, pulling out of Bez's hold and wiping my eyes. "I think I'll stay sober for this one."

"Okay, well—" she looked up at Shadow "—we'll head back to the cottage to spend time with the girls. Call if you need us for anything, okay? We're just across the driveway."

"I will. Thanks." I watched them go before taking a seat on the mattress and inching closer to my mate. "Is Charlotte going to come see him?"

Rebel huffed a laugh. "It took me over an hour to convince her to take the bedtime shift with Eli. You won't be able to keep her away once he goes down for the night."

I nodded, still feeling as if a piece of our puzzle was missing. "And Sariel—"

"She'll be here," Bez said, leaving no room for doubt. "We'll all be here."

"Like a party." I swallowed hard, fighting to keep the tears from falling. To keep the panic at bay. "So… Tonight should be fun."

"Just the eight of us waiting for Julian to wake up and try to kick our asses in his confusion." Rebel pulled up the desk chair, sitting down hard before kicking up his feet on the edge of the bed. "Should have brought some playing cards."

Bez huffed. "The last time we all played cards, Julian and Angelita won every hand."

"They cheated." Rebel shot a wink my way. "Tell him."

I shrugged, my focus on Julian. The man who could tell by someone's breathing pattern if they'd gotten excited. That and the fact that he could hear the rustle of someone squirming in their seat came in handy when playing cards. "We didn't cheat. Julian's just that good."

And he was.

And he would be again.

I just had to stay patient.

NINETEEN

Julian

WHEN ANGELITA HAD BITTEN me the first time, the one to claim me as her mate, I'd thought the colors and light that had exploded in my mind were some of the prettiest I'd ever remembered seeing. I'd been so wrong.

The pictures that screamed through my head as Angelita bit me the second time? Stunning. Magnificent. Striking. They created entire worlds in seas of blues and reds, brought down from the heavens to sink into a blanket of green. I watched for minutes or hours, lost in their changing patterns. In the way they threw light all across my field of vision. It wasn't until the brightness faded that the true nature of the gift she'd given me shone through.

I didn't just see light. I saw shadows. Shapes. And there, on the edge, stood the figure of a girl I'd know anywhere even though I'd never seen her before. I knew those curves, the attitude she held in every inch of her body. I would know my mate even though a pinkish-purple light bathed her in its vibrant aura. So much more dynamic than anything normal senses could see.

My God, nothing would ever be as beautiful as my Angelita.

Time stuttered, stopping and starting as my senses changed course. Colors faded and light darkened, but still, Angelita stood to one side. Always in that same pinkish-purple. Always close. If I strained, I could hear her whispered words, but it took too much energy, so I sought comfort in her shadow and let the changes move over me. She stood guard, it seemed, never leaving my side. Protective of me.

The first sign that my mind had been invaded by another being was a brush of fur against me. Not on my skin, not outside my body—inside it. I could feel the footsteps of an animal moving within my head. Disconcerting, but something told me not to be afraid. Not to fight him. He and I would be joined for the rest of our days, just like Angelita and I. Might as well start off on the right foot.

The wolf made himself at home, sniffing through my memories and thoughts. Playing them back like football tape after a big game. Studying the moments. He whimpered when he found the place where I stored the loss of my parents and my sight. Growled at the remembrances of the battle at Merriweather Fields. But when he got to Angelita? To our hours of talking over the computers and all the time we'd spent together? His growl turned needy, his whine desperate. He liked her. He wanted her. Needed to see her with his own eyes and take in her scent. I couldn't blame him.

What had to be hours passed that way, long bouts of nothing, and then the wolf would move or sniff out something else to learn. Sometimes quiet words caught my attention from somewhere outside my body, or the colors would light up brighter than before. It never mattered what woke me from my sleep-like state, I always searched out one thing. My Angelita in the bright light. My heart and half of my soul. I always found her.

My wolf found her too. She riveted him, held his attention like nothing else could. A protective feeling cocooned us when he watched her, a need to keep her close and safe. To bed down with her in a warm den and block out the rest of the world. He and I would get along just fine.

I sent thoughts to my wolf, ones of *yes, ours,* and *must protect.* Random things to know about her, about us. He absorbed all of it, his feeling of impatience growing the entire time. I felt the same—I wanted to get back to my mate. To wake up and tell her all that had happened. To figure out how to shift so the wolf inside me could get to know her in his own way.

It wasn't until much later that a voice broke through my fuzzy thoughts clear as day. One I'd follow anywhere.

"Come back to me, Julian."

Angelita. I pushed at my mind, shoving past the haze of my subconscious. It hung heavy and thick, almost wrapping itself around me. Tangling me in its foggy clutches. The wolf jumped in with me, clawing at the tattered edges of our shared world until he dug his way back to crisp, clear reality. Working together for the sole purpose of reaching our mate.

I came to fast, needing to relieve the fear I'd heard in Angelita's voice. But when I opened my eyes, I froze. Colors. Still. Not shapes really, not anything as vibrant as what I saw in my head, but definitely something. I'd expected blackness with spots of gray where bright lights shone. Instead, colors bandied about the room, across the ceiling, and down over the edge of the mattress. And still, there sat a shadow of a girl inside a pinkish-purple light. My mate.

For the first time since he appeared, my wolf worked against me. He wanted me to shift so he could take control, wanted to meet his mate. Thankfully, he listened when I thought *wait* to him. He didn't like it, but he took the direction. I made sure he knew he'd get his turn, but first…

"Leelee."

She jumped, her head flying back. That shadow blocked

her face, made it so I couldn't see her features, but I didn't need to. I knew her. And I loved her.

"Hey." She grabbed my hand and leaned closer. "How do you feel?"

I couldn't resist her. I reached up and cupped her cheek, staring at that shadow she threw. "You're so pink."

Her head cocked, and I laughed. That one would need an explanation.

"Seems to have come through okay," Rebel said, his voice moving closer. He didn't glow like Angelita, didn't cast the same sort of shadow either, but I suddenly knew with a surety I hadn't felt in ages where he stood. How he moved. "How're you feeling, kid?"

"Good. I'm good." I sat up and stretched, letting my senses take in the rest of the room. The rest of Rebel's property. The beast inside allowed it…for a little bit. "But my wolf wants me to shift. He wants to meet his mate."

"He wanted something, and you were able to hold him back?" Bez. In the far corner, on his feet, resting one shoulder against the wall. The scratch of fabric against drywall gave him away.

"I didn't have to hold him back. I told him to wait, and he settled down."

"Well, that's a first," Rebel said. "You ever hear of that sort of control?"

Bez grunted. "With mated pairs, sure, but these two haven't been mated long enough to build their bond up like what I've seen in the past. The wolf should have been able to overwhelm Julian without a moment's pause."

I shrugged, still staring at Angelita's glow. "We have a common goal."

Angelita leaned in, the glow growing stronger. Brighter. Happier? "And what's that shared goal?"

"Keeping you safe and warm and close. That's it. It's all we both want."

Rebel sighed. "You two never did do things quite the way we expected."

"That they didn't." Bez stepped toward the door, a heavy shadow pulling across Angelita's light as he distanced himself from her. "Call your team. Let's take these two on a run."

"Sure thing," Rebel said before grabbing my shoulder. "Glad you made it through, kid. Your sister would have had my balls if anything had gone wrong."

"She's had your balls for years," Angelita said with a giggle.

"Truer words have never been spoken. We'll give you two a few minutes while we wrangle some guards for a run. Holler if you need us, though."

The second the door closed behind him, I grabbed Angelita and pulled her in for a long, deep kiss. Licked between her lips and plunged my tongue in deep. She tasted sweet, like candy, and the feel of her skin touching mine sent rockets shooting up my spine. Every sense had increased with the addition of my wolf, every nerve overfiring and drowning me in feelings. But in that moment, with my mate's body warming mine and her taste on my tongue, all that extra input seemed like a blessing. One I would never not be grateful for.

"God, I love you." I bit her jaw, licking and sucking my way to her neck. "I want you so fucking bad."

"Run first," she said, moaning slightly, as if the idea of being around the Feral Breed Motorcycle Club sounded as frustrating to her as it did to me. "I want to see your wolf."

"He wants to see you. So much." I yanked her closer, lifting her so she straddled my lap. She took over from there, rocking her hips against mine, riding the ridge of my hard cock. "What happened to the run?"

"We'll get there." She rocked harder, pressing deeper as

electricity raced through every cell within my body. I'd never felt anything like it, never been so close to losing control so soon.

I gripped her hips, my throaty growl puncturing the relative silence around us. "You're going to make me come."

"That's the whole idea."

So I did. I came right there in my shorts with Angelita falling right along with me. Came with a groan that shook the bed and matched my mate's. The pleasure detonated throughout my mind, rocking me to the very foundation of my being before building me back up. Angelita clung to me, arching and curling her body into mine. And when we finished, when the pulsing completion of our little bump and grind finally quieted, she kissed me, even biting my lip and growling under her breath.

She grabbed my face, holding me still. Looking into my eyes until I could feel her gaze. "So pink, huh?"

"Pink and purple, really. I don't have a name for the color, but it's yours. And your shape—a shadow of you." I ran a finger over her cheek, unable not to touch her. "That's what I can see."

Angelita stiffened. "Is that okay? I mean…I didn't expect you to see anything just because of the turning, but this…it's sort of…"

"A blessing." And I'd never think of it as anything less. I didn't need the see the colors or shadows, not really. But I'd be grateful for them every time I got to let my eyes roam over my mate, no matter what sort of input came through. "Anytime I get to see even just the outline of your body is amazing."

"So you want to see my body?" she asked, her voice teasing as hell.

I wasn't in the mood to tease, though. I tangled my fingers in her hair so I could pull her back to my lips. My mouth. Sliding between her lips for more of her sweetness until she pushed me back.

"Fuchsia," she said. Gasping. Wanting to go again. Wanting more. Fuck, I understood that so much.

But first… "What?"

"Bright pinkish-purple. Fuchsia is a name for that sort of color."

"Huh." I bit her jaw simply because I could. "Fuchsia it is, then, mate."

She shivered, her hands gripping tight. Her body warming as I ran my teeth toward her ear. "We need to run."

"We do, and then…" I licked up the length of her neck, letting my wolf come through. Letting him scent her, taste her. His throaty growl vibrated through my chest, making Angelita freeze.

"Julian?"

She had no reason to fear my wolf. "Run first, alone time later. Your smell, your taste, the way your body brushes mine… Everything feels just a little different, a little more intense. I want to test that in various positions to make sure I'm right."

"That sounds like a lot of testing."

I grinned and pulled her in for another kiss. "If it takes all night, I'll get it done. You'd better not run too hard, Leelee. You're going to need your energy."

She hopped off the bed with a laugh, heading for the door. "Why don't you go ahead and shift, Julian? I'll get us outside."

My wolf didn't need to be told twice, and neither did I. He'd been patient…it was his turn to take over. I wasn't sure what to expect—a need to search for him, a fight between us as he took control—but if there was supposed to be some learning curve to move from one form to another, we didn't need it. One second, I sat on the bed in my human skin. The next, I stood on all fours, covered in fur and adjusting to wolf senses. His sight matched mine but had the brightness and detail level of my unconscious state. Scents, though…sounds. So much stronger, even more than I'd expected. Everything around me smelled like sex and our mate, something that made me whine. Made us want to roll around the mattress to make our fur carry that same scent. To let the other wolves know Angelita belonged to us. To stake our claim.

"C'mon, Julian." Angelita sounded so happy, so relieved. It was a tone I wanted to hear for the rest of our lives. So I prodded at my wolf and made sure he understood—we had one job, and it started and ended with her. If his answering chuff was any indication, he was completely on board.

"Are you coming?" My girl had stepped outside, taking her fuchsia light with her. "I want to run with you. Just wait until you feel the earth under your paws."

She wanted to run as wolves, so we would. Hell, we'd chase her all through the woods if that made her happy. Because at the end of the day, she'd given us so much more than we could ever repay her for. But we'd never stop trying.

So with a yip, we dove off the bed and raced outside. Chasing after the one woman we wanted to catch.

Following the fuchsia.

EPILOGUE

Six Months Later

Angelita

"WHERE DO YOU WANT this?" Scarlett pointed to the box of research books one of the Feral Breed prospects carried, raising an eyebrow. "I bet they're heavy. I mean, I'm not finding out because Shadow would kill me for picking that up in my delicate condition, but they seem heavy."

She'd been using that "delicate condition" line since she found out she was pregnant three months ago. The next half a year was going to be long.

"You can put them here." I grabbed the three laptops sitting on the walnut monstrosity we'd be calling a desk and moved them to a safer location so the prospect—Pup, of course, since every prospect carried that name until they'd earned their patch—lugged the box over.

Scarlett smiled at the prospect and directed him back downstairs before turning and inspecting the books. "Coding, electrical wiring, HVAC—these look like vocational school textbooks."

"They are."

"Why do you have them?"

"Because sometimes I need to be creative to find a way

inside. Or don't you remember that first job when you blew the power to the building for me?"

"Oh, right. Good times." She shot me a wink, her red lips pulling up into a small smile. "Though from what I hear, finding a creative way inside is Julian's skill."

My cheeks burned, and I tried to shrug off her raised eyebrow. "We're newly mated, and he's still not always in control of his wolf."

Both true, both probably affecting his sex drive. But really, I gave no fucks for how loud or rough or often we had sex. My mate had grown since his turning, adding a handful of inches and some serious pounds of solid muscle. Where wolves like Rebel, Bez, and Shadow tended to have a leaner frame, Julian bulked similar to Phoenix. He looked like some sort of body builder—not the scary ones, but the hot as fuck ones dropping pics on Instagram. Yeah. My man made women drool. Who could blame me for wanting to ride that at all hours of the day and night?

But apparently, our mating had become a problem when Rebel and Charlotte no longer felt comfortable walking into their own garage, so we were in the process of moving both our home and our business.

That's right—our *business*. Five item-recovery jobs booked and completed after that first bear shifter one, and we'd officially opened our doors to clients. Harley and Shiloh's word-of-mouth campaign had definitely helped. We'd been busy retrieving items for bear-shifter clans and had four more cases waiting to be worked on. At that rate, I'd need to hire help soon just to keep up.

I still couldn't get over the rush of pride when I thought of how much we'd accomplished already. Rebel had rented us a storefront on the corner of his denhouse in the city, and Beast had found us a townhouse for rent just a few blocks away. The setup seemed perfect—easy commute, a neighborhood we knew and loved, plus all the Feral Breed guys around to jump in if we needed backup. What more could I ask for?

Scarlett suddenly spun, staring out the door like a kid waiting for Santa Claus. "Ooh, I hear Shadow. Our mates must be back."

Okay, I could always ask for more time with my mate. I set down the files I'd been about to put away and hurried to the front of the desk. "You should probably go meet him. Not that I'm kicking you out or anything." I was totally kicking her out. Luckily, Scarlett never seemed to get offended when I dismissed her so I could get my mate alone.

"Subtle, kid. Real subtle." She pinched my arm teasingly on her way toward the door. "I can take a hint, though. We'll leave you and your boy toy alone for a bit. Pretty sure the prospects are tired of carrying your shit all across town anyway."

Her words barely registered because at that moment, three men walked in the front door and strode down the hall toward us. Julian led the way, his dark sunglasses in place and his stride long. Heavy boots hit the wood floor in a rhythm I could feel in my soul, but when he took off his glasses and looked right at me? That thumping turned into a pulse I felt right between my legs. He still couldn't truly see like before the accident that took his parents, but his vision had returned somewhat in the transition. Colors and shadows was how he explained it—fuchsia for me, specifically. However it manifested, he seemed happy with the change, and I definitely liked the way his eyes followed me whenever he was around. Especially in moments like right now. He'd been to the gym, then on a run with the guys, something they did daily to keep his wolf happy. The animal worked well with Julian but sometimes tried to overpower him when presented with something his animal instincts found appealing. Like food…or me.

And right now, I could see the hunger in Julian's eyes, the need. His wolf was close to the surface, which called to mine. That animalistic edge also always led to great sex.

Game on.

"C'mon boys," Scarlett said, intercepting the crew and directing Shadow and Rebel back toward the door. "Let's leave these two alone so they can figure out what files go in which drawers."

"Pretty sure they figured that out a while ago." Rebel lifted a chin, smiling my way. "Come on over to the den when you're ready for more help. I like to keep my prospects busy."

I nodded but said nothing, too enraptured by the look on Julian's face. Too aroused to deal with others. And when they shut the door behind them, leaving Julian and me alone, I took my chance.

Smiling, I hopped up onto the edge of the desk and crossed my legs. "Welcome to Feral Breed Bounty Hunters. How may I be of service?"

Julian quirked an eyebrow. "Are you offering to service me, mate?"

Fuck, those words should not have made me as wet as they did. Of course, it helped that Julian had reached the desk. He wasted no time grabbing my legs and spreading them around his thick thighs, opening me up for him. Dominating me in the best possible way.

I dragged a heel across his ass, pulling us tighter together. "I'm always offering."

Rough hands stroked my thighs, warming me. He smelled like rain and forest as he leaned closer. Smelled like mine. "How do you want it?"

"Hard." I grunted when he yanked me closer, his thick fingers already pulling on the edge of my panties. "And right here."

"You want to christen our desk?"

"I want to remember you fucking me on this desk every time we're quietly working across from one another." I pushed him off me, just enough so I could roll over. So I could bend across the desk with my ass in the air. A position I knew would drive his wolf crazy, making Julian's actions harsher, more aggressive. Hotter.

He didn't disappoint. Callused hands tore my panties even before he flipped up the soft skirt I wore. So close to losing control. So close to simply taking what he wanted. But Julian always thought of me first—of my needs and desires. So instead of simply taking, he teased. Smacking my ass with his heavy hand, making me jump, making my pussy grow wetter with a sharp slice of pain that melted into pure pleasure.

"You like when I do that, mate?"

I loved it, but I didn't need to tell him that. He knew. He always knew.

With a growl that had me shaking all over, Julian pressed a finger inside me, rumbling in his throat. "Fuck, you're soaked already. I love that you're always so wet for me."

I grappled to hold on to the edge of the desk, lifting my hips for more. "Only for you."

The growl he released almost drowned out the sound of him removing his belt and unzipping his jeans. I waited, knowing he'd grab his heavy cock and stroke it once, maybe twice, before lining himself up. Before nudging the thick head across my clit. Before thrusting home.

But he shocked me by leaning forward to kiss the back of my neck with a sweetness that stole my breath. "Love you, Leelee."

I grabbed his hand and pulled him closer, tugging his arm around me. "Forever, Julian. We're going to have the best forever."

And it would be. He'd come through the turning safely and more in tune with his wolf than anyone Bez or Rebel had ever seen, we had a home, and our business of recovering things lost or stolen for whatever paranormals could pay the fee supported us. Julian would go back to school next semester, transferring to Wayne State to stay close. And me?

My love for Julian had turned me into a thief, and I couldn't be more grateful for that fact. Together, we could do anything. Together, we'd finally get our happily ever after.

A moment of fate interrupted by danger.

The story that started it all.

FERAL BREED MOTORCYCLE CLUB

BOOK ONE

ACKNOWLEDGMENTS

This book was a long time coming. Three years, to be exact. From the time I wrote *Claiming His Fate*, I knew Julian would have his own story. But at the end of *Claiming His Desire*, he and Angelita were still just teenagers. Babies in my head. I needed to give them time to grow up and show me who they were inside. When I wrote *Baby Mine*, I realized it was close to time to revisit my young mates. It took me another year to wrap my head around their story and finish it. That was a long process, so I hope I gave them the story they deserved.

It wouldn't be a Feral Breed book without the input of my friend, my favorite bad influence, my editor, and my fellow Flavor Town member, Lisa Hollett. Thank you, Lisa, for always laughing at my pirate speak. You're the only one who does.

To the readers who hang out in my reader group. You ladies rock my socks off. Judy, Terry, Ingrid, Fran, Angi, Teri, Mary, Tonya, Karen, Felicia, Kimberly, Beth, Shelly, Jackie, Jennifer, Kim, Lisa, Donna, CJ, Jessie, Debby, and all the people I'm probably forgetting. Thank you all for sticking with me.

A special thanks to Eileen Friel who named my bear shifters for me. YOU ROCK!

Last but not least, thank you to my little family. Without my husband or kids, I have on idea what I'd do with myself. Probably sleep more. Definitely sleep more.

But life wouldn't be anywhere near as fun.

ABOUT THE AUTHOR

A storyteller from the time she could talk, Ellis grew up among family legends of hauntings, psychics, and love spanning decades. Those stories didn't always have the happiest of endings, so they inspired her to write about real life, real love, and the difficulties therein. From farmers to werewolves, store clerks to witches—if there's love to be found, she'll write about it. Ellis lives in the Chicago area with her husband, daughters, and a German Shepherd that refuses to leave her side.

Find Ellis online at:
Website: www.ellisleigh.com
Twitter: https://twitter.com/ellis_writes
Facebook: https://www.facebook.com/ellisleighwrites

Edited by Silently Correcting Your Grammar, LLC
Cover Art by Cormar Covers